CON
OVER THE
HILL

A perfect feel-good read from one
of Britain's best-loved authors

NICHOLAS RHEA

Constable Nick Mystery Book 36

Revised edition 2022
Joffe Books, London
www.joffebooks.com

First published in Great Britain in 2011
by Robert Hale Limited

This paperback edition was first published
in Great Britain in 2022

ISBN: 978-1-80405-257-0

CHAPTER 1

One morning in late spring, I received a telephone call from Inspector Harry Breckon. He was in charge of Eltering sub-division which includes the whole of Ashfordly section, Aidensfield and all the villages which formed my beat. He was calling from his office.

'Ah, Nick,' he said. He was a very pleasant man with a penchant for making political speeches, but I had a lot of respect for him. 'I need to have a chat with you. Where are you patrolling today?'

I gave him a brief outline of my anticipated route, bearing in mind some of the calls I had to make to check stock registers, renew firearms certificates and take statements from people who had witnessed crimes or traffic accidents in other police areas.

'Hmm,' he said. 'I have to pay a visit to Ashfordly Police Station this morning to return some court files, and then I'd like to see you. I need to have a chat with you alone, not in a police station where the walls have ears. Constabulary ears do tend to flap a lot. How about Aidensfield Beacon? It's remote up there and it's a fine, calm day so we won't get swept away by the wind or get our caps blown off. We could have a nice cosy chat. Say twelve thirty?'

1

'Yes, sir, that would be fine.'

'OK, see you there unless something dramatic happens in the meantime. Radio me if you can't make it. I'll be out and about in my car.'

Needless to say, for the rest of that morning I pondered the reason for this unexpected summons.

I tried to recall the cases I had recently dealt with, the reports I had submitted and the statements I had completed for other police forces. It sounded as if I had committed a major error that now required a confidential meeting—interviews with senior officers, especially those away from flapping ears, usually meant trouble and the need to produce a humiliating explanation of some kind. That morning's patrolling was, therefore, not a very happy experience as my mind struggled to find a reason for the impending rendezvous.

I arrived at Aidensfield Beacon a few minutes ahead of the appointed time to find the inspector already there. It was fine, sunny weather and he was standing outside his official car admiring the view that embraced almost an entire 360 degrees; from there, we could see all the main Yorkshire uplands—the North York Moors, the Pennines and Dales besides the Wolds of the East Riding. The site provides some of the finest views in Yorkshire.

'Ah, Nick.' He was such a warm and friendly man that he could use our forenames without seeming too casual. Most senior officers addressed us by our surnames only. 'Glad you could make it. And what a view, eh? I'm surprised there isn't a tourist car park and viewing point up here.' I noticed he was carrying a file of papers.

'All in good time, sir!' I quipped. 'It's already happening at some of our other vantage points on the moors. The tourists are taking over, they seem to be everywhere and nowadays, things are planned especially to accommodate them. The Highways Authorities are even creating cycle lanes especially for tourists on bikes—they never did that for ordinary people or children going to school.'

'It keeps us all in work, Nick. Tourism is good for the area; it brings in much-needed money even if most of us do complain. Now to the reason for this meeting. You enjoy working the Aidensfield beat, I believe? And not only for views like this?'

'I do, sir. It's a wonderful and very picturesque part of Yorkshire in which to work—the people are very decent and helpful to the police. The work is varied and always interesting. My wife and children like it here, too. They've made lots of friends and the school is very good so the posting is ideal in all sorts of ways.'

'There's not a lot of crime to deal with either,' he made that comment with a slight frown on his face. Maybe I should have realized the frown meant something not very pleasant. 'In fact, Nick, I'd say the crime figures for Aidensfield are the lowest in the force area. What have you recorded this year? Let's have a look,' and, as if to stem any answer from me, he opened the file he was carrying.

He read from it. 'Theft of some farm equipment for which you apprehended the thief, an indecent assault on a teenage girl walking to the bus—and you caught the offender. An alleged rape which turned out not to be a rape but more of a frolic in the woods that the girl later regretted . . . The theft of a car for which no one has been arrested. Another car dumped on your patch after being stolen in Hull and the thief helped himself to a vehicle from your pub car park. The same vehicle was found later in Stockton-on-Tees, but no thief was traced. The theft of some tomato plants from a greenhouse, even a bit of old rope stolen . . . Aidensfield is not exactly the crime centre of Yorkshire, is it?'

'That's why it's such a pleasant beat, sir.' I tried to produce a spirited response. 'After all, isn't the hallmark of good policing a constantly low crime rate? That's what crime prevention is all about, especially on a rural beat.'

'I can't argue against that, Nick.'

'Well, sir, you'll know that on a rural beat like Aidensfield, it's all to do with the constable being seen in uniform at the times and places where crime is most likely to happen—and then preventing the occurrence of anything criminal.'

'A fine speech and, as I've just said, I couldn't agree more, but we must heed the statistics.'

'Figures don't reveal everything, sir.' I felt I had to make my point because I could feel he was leading to something that would require a full explanation from me. 'Prevention of crime is one of our most important duties and I reckon my presence and my system of patrolling have kept the figures low on Aidensfield beat.'

'As I've already said, Nick, no one would dispute that.'

'The important thing, sir, is to appreciate that quite simply, those low crime figures depend upon the constant presence of the local constable who can always be seen patrolling his beat and who might turn up at any unexpected time, day or night, and in any place.'

'Unfortunately, Nick, that kind of logic doesn't convince our political leaders. And we do have a Labour government in power, don't forget.'

Here comes one of his speeches, I thought.

'They're renowned for thinking politically rather than considering things from a common-sense point of view. They base their judgments on statistics, league tables and other forms of target-based rationale, rather than letting the quality of work speak for itself.'

'So what are you telling me, sir?'

'The government is putting pressure on the entire British police service, Nick. It's doing it through the Home Office with the intention of reducing costs.'

'That's always been the case, sir, I used to work in the accounts office at Force Headquarters, so I know how the system works.'

'Then you'll understand what I am saying. But enough of my preaching! The reason I'm here is because the authorities have turned their attention to rural beats. The Home Office is compelling every police force to evaluate their rural beats, taking into account the number and types of crimes committed per annum, the number of crimes and offences detected, the number of indictable and summary offences processed in the courts, the number of traffic accidents and fatalities, the number of sudden deaths dealt with by the police, outbreaks of contagious diseases of animals, the population of the beats, the cost of actually running each beat with a resident constable in a police-owned house . . . in fact everything connected with your duties and all the incidents you are likely to deal with.'

'And the reason for this, sir?'

'Cost, Nick. As we know, it costs a lot of money to run and administer a rural beat—the constable's wages and uniform, the upkeep of the police house and its attached office, police transport, official telephone calls, statutory allowances . . . it all adds up. Rural bobbies don't come cheap. The Home Office argument is that a high percentage of rural beats throughout England and Wales could be amalgamated with neighbouring beats. Two, three or even four could be merged to form a larger unit served by just one constable using a radio-equipped motor vehicle. He could be supported by neighbouring constables similarly equipped, working around the clock in eight-hour shifts. With modern transport and up-to-date communications, it's a feasible suggestion according to the Home Office. Such constables would then be posted to areas where there is a high crime rate and a shortage of beat officers. In those places, there'd be more work to occupy them; lots of rural beats would be closed down, the police houses and vehicles sold. Thus the taxpayers and rate-payers will not be paying over the odds for their policing. The official line is that vast savings will be made without impairing efficiency and that the public will derive great benefit from an updated rural police presence. The reality is that we shall have to do the same job for less money and there'll be no increase in our public presence. In fact, of course, there'll be fewer constables in rural areas.'

'I'd have thought, sir, that to police more efficiently, we need *more* money and *more* officers, not fewer. Surely, the cost of maintaining police numbers would be offset by the reduction in crime—crime costs us money too. Politicians seem to forget that. The real cost of crime rarely appears in the equation.'

'That's what all police officers think too, but sadly we're not politicians and we have no power to contradict them. Like it or not, they are our masters. We're stuck with them, good or bad.'

I knew the police service was funded half by Government and half by local rate-payers, but sometimes official number-crunching and statistics could conceal the truth. If rural beats were closed and the police houses sold, a lot of people in rural areas would feel let down at the least or vulnerable to crime and vandalism at the worst. The village constable in his local police house was a form of insurance that created a general feeling of comfort and security. It didn't matter to the public that he often patrolled in his uniform without apparently doing a lot—effective policing is not apparently productive, like factory work.

There was no doubt that, without the constable living in the village, crime and disorder would increase, particularly acts of petty vandalism, rowdiness, damage and general misbehaviour.

Anti-social behaviour is not always classed as a crime, but it is a worrying and sometimes a frightening nuisance to anyone targeted by yobs. It was that kind of lawlessness that the public disliked because, if unchecked, it frequently led to more serious offences.

'We know this is a political ploy, Nick, but that's how politicians operate—it won't save money, the public won't like it, but it will look splendid in the Labour government's statistics. They will make all sorts of exaggerated claims and trot out all sorts of wonderful statistics to prove they are a good Government. That's all that concerns them—not the reality of the situation.'

By this stage, I was wondering how all this would affect me—I was sure the inspector hadn't summoned me to this hilltop merely for an excuse to talk politics. He was preparing the path for an announcement of some kind.

'You'll be wondering what all this has to do with you?' he said, as if he were reading my thoughts.

'Well, yes, sir, I was.'

'I have to tell you, Nick, that the chief constable, in light of pressure from the Home Office, proposes to close several rural beats in the North Riding. Sadly, Aidensfield is one of them. With its low crime rate and very light workload, there is no justification for maintaining a full-time resident police presence in the village. Aidensfield could be served quite efficiently from Ashfordly Police Station or it could be staffed by amalgamating it with other rural beats. The finer details have yet to be worked out but the chief constable thought you should be informed at this early stage, bearing in mind you have a young family. You will need to start planning for a transfer elsewhere—packing your inessential belongings, little-used furniture and so forth. Tell your bank, children's school, people living and working on your beat and generally preparing people for the time when they haven't got a village constable. There is a high probability that you will be transferred from Aidensfield within the next two or three months.'

I was shocked and speechless. After all my efforts to keep the village free of crime it now seemed my work was to have no further effect. For what seemed a long time, I did not reply to Inspector Breckon. I was too engrossed with my own thoughts, considering all the people on my patch with whom I and my family had struck up valued friendships, wondering how Mary and the children would react, wondering about schools or where I was likely to be posted . . . it was rather like someone kicking my legs from under me.

'Is the decision final?' I heard myself ask. 'About the closure of Aidensfield?'

'Yes, Nick. Mounting a challenge would be a waste of time. The decision has already been made. Of all the beats in our Force area—the whole of the North Riding in fact— yours has the lowest crime rate and the smallest workload.'

'So I've worked myself out of a job?'

'It happens, Nick. Sadly, it happens.'

'So where am I to be posted? Has that been decided?'

'Not yet. That's the second reason for this chat. The chief constable wants to see you in his office at Headquarters. Next Monday morning, eleven o'clock on the dot: best uniform, smart haircut, polished boots, pressed trousers, no fluff or dandruff on your tunic . . . you know the drill.'

'Yes, sir,' was all I could think of saying as my heart sunk into my boots. So I was going to leave Aidensfield . . . and if Inspector Breckon was correct in what he was saying, Aidensfield would never again be a police officer's rural beat.

My own—admittedly biased—view, was that this village was a beat populated with perhaps the most decent and interesting people in the land. It had a police house with one of the finest views in the country, the dramatic countryside around it was beautiful and it had provided me with some of my happiest times in the service. It was my beat. My very own patch of England and home to me and my growing family.

He interrupted my musings by saying, 'Oh, and another thing, Nick. This morning when I was in Ashfordly, I got a complaint from a woman who said she was an RSPCA member. She had seen Claude Jeremiah Greengrass using a cart drawn by a dog. It was on a lane near Briggsby. I went to see if he was still there as I drove to meet you, but there was no sign of him. You'd better check out the tale—you know that using a dog to draw a cart on the public highway is illegal as a form of cruelty?'

'Yes, sir, it's in the Protection of Animals Act of 1911. I'll deal with the matter.'

'She was called Susan Potiphar, odd sort of spelling if you ask me.'

'I know her, she lives in Aidensfield. She often makes complaints if she thinks animals are being cruelly treated.'

'Good, I'll let you go now so you can deal with that and I will expect an offence report from you in due course.

Another crime for your statistics! Detected, of course! With a prosecution to follow.'

'I'll sort it out, sir. It will be recorded as detected before I leave Aidensfield,' and I managed a sad smile.

I stood alone with my thoughts on that hill top for a long, long time after the inspector had driven off. So all this would no longer be my very own beat.

Now I had the task of informing Mary and the children.

CHAPTER 2

I decided not to tell Mary my news until the children were tucked up in bed and fast asleep. I wanted her reaction without the inevitable questions from our four offspring who were increasingly interested in listening to adult conversations and relating everything to themselves and their school friends. They loved to emphasize their own views and opinions while raising all types of awkward queries. But, of course, every query had to be answered. Our family had increased from three to four during my spell at Aidensfield—we now had three fast-growing girls and one boy. I recall one of the girls asking, 'Daddy, are you a good policeman?'

'Yes, I think so,' was my confident response.

'Then why don't you arrest all the bad people?' It was a good question.

With my news still a secret and the children safely in bed, Mary and I went into the front lounge with its incredible long-distance views over stunningly beautiful countryside. I put some more fuel on the fire and settled down for our usual evening chat and assessment of our days' activities over a cup of tea and a biscuit. We'd had our evening meal earlier, with the family—we always made a point of eating our main meals together around the table. Being late spring, it was still daylight, if a little chilly, hence the need for a coal fire.

Mary was relaxed after her day—she wore comfortable dark blue trousers, a cosy light blue sweater and slippers whereas I, having to remind myself that even though my shift was complete, remained in uniform. Mine was a twenty-four hour responsibility as far as serious matters were concerned, however, I had removed my uniform tunic and sat down in my police shirt and trousers, plus my big black boots. I was superstitious about removing my boots in favour of comfortable slippers.

I could almost guarantee that if I did put on my slippers, I would be called out to an emergency of some kind—minor problems could wait. Even after leaving the police service, it took me a long time to overcome that old and ingrained belief. Very rarely did I don my slippers before going to bed just in case there was a knock on the door or a phone call that demanded my presence elsewhere. The problem was that on several occasions when I had removed my boots and donned my slippers for the evening, I had been called out to a variety of incidents. It was as if the removal of my boots triggered incidents such as fights in pubs, domestic battles between spouses, traffic accidents or reports of theft and suspicious characters seen wandering behind the cottages of the villages on my patch. I suspected they'd be pimping, or even looking for light and easy pickings in the form of vegetables, fruit and flowers from back gardens. Despite the formal shift of eight hours, therefore, I was never really off duty—not even when I wore my slippers or was tucked up in bed.

So that evening, as on most evenings, I sat with my boots on, just in case. Being on call also meant I could not enjoy a drink of beer in those relaxing moments—it would be dreadful if the village constable arrived at the scene of an incident smelling of alcohol—it would present a bad image. I therefore permitted myself just a small drink of wine unless I was enjoying a full day off duty with my patch being looked after by another officer. What that meant, of course, was that while wearing my police boots I would always be cautious of alcohol. Those boots were a good *aide-mémoire*.

We operated a system where the constables patrolling Ashfordly would cover for us when we were off duty after completing a full shift. They had a huge patch to patrol though, and it could almost be guaranteed that if I or my colleagues wanted urgent assistance, our workmates would be twenty miles away dealing with something else. And if something happened in Aidensfield, it was almost inevitable that I would receive the first call about it. As a consequence, it was often easier for me to turn out to finalize the matter—and, of course, the public deserved a rapid response especially if the matter was serious.

Comfortably settled for that evening, however, I was about to impart my important news to Mary when she said, with a hint of pride in her voice, 'Nick, you'll never guess what's happened.'

'Go on, surprise me,' I said.

'It's Charles, he sat a test at school last week. It was a routine test for seven-year-olds, a mixture of maths, English, geography, history and so forth, but the results are studied by the Headmaster of Elsinby Castle.'

Elsinby Castle was the preparatory school for Maddleskirk College, the leading Roman Catholic public school in Britain and perhaps the best in the world. The castle, the oldest part of which dates to the reign of Edward II (1284-1327), was on my beat and I was a regular caller, often popping in for a quick coffee while dealing with some small incident or providing advice as part of my general patrolling. The castle is believed to contain construction work dating from every century since it was built and it is occasionally open to the public. The prep school accepted boys from the age of eight to eleven, after which they were moved across the valley to Maddleskirk College, the senior part of the school with its first-class reputation for superior education. Run by monks of the Benedictine Order, it was a private school with very high fees and costly term expenses, but it did produce some remarkable results with a high percentage of its pupils going up to either Oxford or Cambridge University.

'Why would the Headmaster of Elsinby Castle be interested in the results of a test for seven-year-olds in our local primary school?' I asked.

'They've got a few places for exceptional pupils. If any boy gets more than 80 per cent, he's considered good enough to be a candidate for entry into the prep school—but he must also take another exam set by that school. Those tests sort out the very best of the current candidates. Getting a good result in our village school is the first hurdle, but if he then passes the castle's own exam, he could be awarded a scholarship. To win that, he'd have to be in the top six of that year's hopefuls.'

'A scholarship? To help with the fees you mean?'

'Yes, and it's open to the pupils of our Catholic primary school.'

'But it's not compulsory, is it? The local children aren't forced to sit the Elsinby exam?'

'No, of course not, but the Abbey and College have a special interest in our village school and this is a unique privilege that provides a wonderful opportunity to all the local boys, irrespective of their background and family circumstances.'

'Not girls?'

'Not yet, but there is talk of girls being admitted. Currently ours would be eligible for the Bar Convent in York which takes weekly boarders as well as day pupils. It also has a scholarship scheme and our girls can sit for that when they're ten.'

'Scholarships don't pay for everything, Mary,' I said, 'and even if Charles was successful we'd have a struggle, not necessarily with the fees but coping with all the extra costs.'

'It wouldn't be anything like as expensive as boarding fees, Nick; being awarded one of these scholarships means attending Elsinby Castle Preparatory School as a day-boy so there would be no boarding fees. Remember the scholarships we are talking about are special ones purely for local boys who would attend as day pupils, not boarders. Maddleskirk

College as well as Elsinby Castle, is keen to attract youngsters from ordinary backgrounds who live in the surrounding villages. There's space in both the senior and junior parts of the school for a few day pupils but the prep school fees will only be paid for day-boys who win a scholarship.'

'Forgetting the expense involved, it sounds good to me, Mary. Quite an opportunity by any standards but is it practicable for us. And for Charles?'

'I think so, because once accepted by Elsinby Castle, it guarantees the boy a place in the senior school. There's always a waiting-list, but a place at Elsinby Castle can by-pass that. If he does get one of those scholarships, fees will still have to be paid for the senior school although even the senior school offers some financial help to parents. He could attend the senior school as a day-boy too, and so reduce the fees. We can't ignore this chance, Nick.'

'I realize that but don't forget I'm just a village policeman for heaven's sake,' I reminded her. 'People from our background don't go to private schools. A policeman's wage is hardly enough to keep our family in food and clothes, let alone pay for a private education, or just part of it. We'd have to meet the expenses that go along with that kind of education even if the basic fees were paid through a scholarship.'

'Yes, I know all that, but you're starting to earn something from your writing now, who knows what that might lead to? Remember that if Charles does well in the entrance exam for Elsinby Castle and gets a scholarship, there'd be no fees. That's the whole idea. That's what we are concerned with right now. And he is a bright lad, Nick. It's a chance we have to take. We'd be unlikely to get this kind of opportunity anywhere else. We are very lucky to have this opportunity, we shouldn't forget that.'

'Mary, you know I've always wanted the best possible education for all the children and I'm very aware of the benefits of a private education. But we can't ignore the additional expenses there'd be even if Charles won a scholarship— there'd be extras like music lessons and carpentry; he'd need pocket money, money for outings and so on . . . and the uniform! And if we did that for him, Mary, we'd have to do the same for the girls. You've always said that girls and boys should have equal education.'

'I stick by that,' she emphasized. 'I do want our girls to be well educated. Charles wouldn't be alone in this; we'd have to do something similar for them.'

'Whatever we decide,' I said, 'it can only be the best we can afford. I do believe that if a child has a good education, it can never be taken away from him or her. It's not like buying them a bike or car if they do well, such things don't last forever and are soon forgotten. So I'm prepared to spend money on their education. Also, when it comes to the cost, I suppose it will be spread over several years so we must examine all the aspects very carefully.'

'I know, Nick, but I still think we should let Charles take that entrance exam.'

'And if he passes, what next? Do we let him go to such a posh school? Can we honestly afford it? Anyway if Charles *doesn't* pass the entrance exam—and it will be a tough one— we can forget the whole idea. It's may be just one of those dreams that ambitious parents have, getting their children placed in the best schools.'

'Building Elsinby Castles in the air?' she smiled.

'Something like that. Anyway, I've something to tell you which has a bearing on this.'

'Just a minute,' she interrupted. 'I haven't finished yet. We haven't decided whether he should take the entrance exam. You can't let this go, just like that, as if it's not happening. It's such a wonderful opportunity, Nick, we must discuss it—and all the consequences.'

'There's not a lot more we can discuss at this stage. Charles has passed the first test, he's halfway there. He must take the second one, mustn't he?'

'It's the only basis we would have for making the big decision, Nick. But if he passes and is awarded a scholarship, what then?'

'We sit down and talk it through with him and the girls; he'll really have to *want* to go there, remember, we can't send him if he hates the idea. But this test is for day pupils, remember, so if he goes to Elsinby Castle, it will mean our having to live here or nearby, for the duration of that schooling—until he's eleven. Looking ahead, though, there's no way we can afford the fees for the upper school, even as a day pupil, but especially for boarding,' I stressed. 'That's what I've been trying to tell you.'

'Trying to tell me what?' she frowned and looked concerned. 'Nick, what's happened? You've been preoccupied all evening . . . I don't think you've listened to a word I've said!'

'I've heard every one of them, believe me,' I smiled in an effort to break the tension that was now building up with remarkable speed. What had begun as a cosy evening for two over the fire was now threatening to become a verbal tussle of sorts. 'I just can't see all our children going to posh and expensive private schools, the suggestion's out of our league by a million miles . . .'

'I could get a job,' she volunteered 'The children are growing up . . .'

'Before we go down that route, I want you to halt for just a moment or two and listen to what I have to say,' I spoke with perhaps more sharpness than necessary. 'You must listen to what I am trying to tell you. I had a visit from Inspector Breckon today.'

'And?'

I paused because I didn't really know how to break the news to her especially as she was brimming with happiness and huge expectations for Charles's success in his exam. It seemed I was about to demolish all her dreams.

Then the telephone rang. I groaned—and I hadn't even got around to taking my boots off. It was rather like telling a story in a restaurant: you just get to the punch line when the waiter comes to ask, 'Everything all right, sir?' That intervention is guaranteed to demolish the entire atmosphere. And so it was with this call. But I had to answer it. I hurried through to the office and picked up the handset.

'Aidensfield Police. PC Rhea speaking.'

'Ah, glad I caught you, PC Rhea,' it was a woman's voice. 'It's Susan Potiphar. I'm sorry to ring you in the evening, but I expect you would be out during the day, but it's just that I saw that man Greengrass in a cart towed by a dog. Now, as I am sure you know, Mr Rhea, that is illegal . . . you realize it is cruelty?'

'My inspector has already told me about it, Mrs Potiphar,' I interrupted. 'I shall be interviewing Mr Greengrass when I return to duty tomorrow.'

'I rather thought you might go this evening, Mr Rhea, as this is a very important breach of the law.'

'I have finished my tour of duty for today, Mrs Potiphar, and this is by no means an emergency. I shall visit Mr Greengrass tomorrow to deal with the matter.'

'Oh.'

'I am at home with my family just now, trying to deal with a very important and serious personal matter. If you feel this is a genuine emergency, a matter of life and death, you could ring Ashfordly police and they will send out someone to speak to Claude.'

'Oh, I see, yes of course. I am sure this is no emergency, so tomorrow then?'

'Yes, I'll interview Mr Greengrass tomorrow.'

'Thank you Mr Rhea,' and she rang off.

Mary was waiting for me. I told her about the call, adding it was not an emergency.

'You said you'd had a visit from the inspector. Is something wrong?'

'They're closing Aidensfield beat,' I told her simply.

She didn't reply for a long time then burst out with, 'Closing it? But why, Nick? Why do a thing like that?' I could see the tears welling up in her eyes. 'We're so happy here, so settled, the children love it and are doing well at school, we've all made friends, we are even the 'Policeman's Family' . . . they can't do that, Nick. They can't. Surely?'

'They can,' I spoke softly. 'And they're going ahead, it's more than just a proposal. It's all to do with cost effectiveness and pressure from the Home Office, not to mention the famous exigencies of the service, whatever that means.'

'So what will happen?'

'Aidensfield will be amalgamated with other beats to reduce expenditure while maintaining maximum coverage of the beats.'

'No, I meant what will happen to us, you, me and the children?'

'We'll be moved into another police house in a different part of the county. And at this stage, I don't know where that will be. I don't think it will be another rural beat if they're being closed down—it'll probably be a town, Scarborough, Strensford, Whitby, Richmond . . . anywhere within the North Riding in fact.'

Tears began to well in her eyes. 'I can't believe this, Nick, really I can't, they can't do this to us, not now . . . so when is all this supposed to happen?' she added weakly.

'Within the next two or three months, so I was told. I don't know anything else about it, but I have to report to the chief constable at Police Headquarters at eleven o'clock on Monday morning. He wants to talk to me. I'll know more by then.'

'You've not been misbehaving, have you? They're not closing the beat to teach you a lesson?'

'No, it's nothing like that. Look, Mary, all I know is that Aidensfield beat is scheduled for closure which means I shall be working somewhere else . . . that is a simple fact. Now you know why I wasn't too enthusiastic about Charles passing that exam. Even if he wins a scholarship, I can't see us taking advantage of it. We'll need to live in the locality but I am obliged to live where the Force decides. If the beat is going to close it will certainly mean leaving this house.'

'Oh, Nick, this is dreadful . . . so where might we be living?'

18

'As I said, at the moment I have no idea. Absolutely no idea, probably one of our local towns.'

She did not speak for a while, allowing time for the news to sink in, before continuing. 'No idea? Not even the slightest? But they can't just move us around like cattle to some other part of the county, can they? And plonk us in any old house! In any dirty old town? Surely we have rights . . . we're not policemen, me and the children. Surely we could live here and you could be posted to Timbuctoo or wherever and drive to work every day like a normal person.'

'The police service doesn't operate like that, Mary. It's a disciplined organization and it's stated in my conditions of service that I must agree to serve anywhere within the North Riding of Yorkshire . . .'

By now the tears were flowing like rivers down her cheeks and she sobbed into a handkerchief, 'But I've been so happy here, we all have . . . why should they be able to move us like that. It's so unfair, after all the work you've put in here, night and day, weekends, bank holidays . . . a low crime rate, few complaints from residents about trouble, youngsters behaving themselves . . . and you've always been on call, like you are now . . . so they reward you by transferring you to God-Knows-Where—and that means us going as well. It's all wrong, Nick, all wrong, so unjust.'

Her reaction was entirely to be expected, but I hoped she would be more understanding in time. Despite my own unhappiness at this development, I had to stand firm and remind her that it was my job. Difficult though it was, I tried to become a peacemaker.

'Look, I'll know more on Monday. We can't make any plans until I find out what's going to happen to me.'

'So what are we going to tell the school? Charles has done so well, Nick, he's so bright. Do we let him take the Elsinby Castle exam or not? Is there any point now? We have to let the secretary at Elsinby Castle know by tomorrow.'

I still wasn't sure. If he passed, it would place us in a dreadful dilemma of our own making. It would result in

Charles being offered a place as a day pupil, a prize we could never accept if we had to live away from Aidensfield—quite apart from the expense. I couldn't ignore that. Realistically, it seemed the idea was doomed.

One bonus was that if he did sit the exam, whatever the outcome, it would establish his academic abilities. That could help to prepare us for whatever lay ahead, wherever it might be. Irrespective of my own career, I began to come around to the idea that taking the exam would be of great benefit to both him and us. It would be a sort of barometer by which to gauge the future. I could not omit the fact that we would have to discuss it with Charles too; after all, he might not want to attend such a posh school. It would be a very difficult decision for a lad of only seven years to make. But I had a decision to make—now.

'Let's encourage him to sit the exam if he wants to. I don't want him to feel under any compulsion,' I conceded. 'We've a few days before Monday then there'll be a couple of months or so before we have to vacate this house. I suppose, if I was totally disenchanted with it all, I could pack in police work and do something else. I've no qualifications, though, but that doesn't matter. I've my own abilities and confidence in myself . . . I could get by until something better came along. I could even clean windows if necessary or sell double-glazing. So yes, Mary, let's see what Charles is made of. The very least it can do is to give us a starting point for the next stage of our family life. When will we know the result?'

'He sits the exam on Monday . . . while you're at Headquarters seeing the chief constable. I think the results will be out before the following weekend.'

The exam would be a tough one—it had to be so because it was designed to weed out those who would never cope with the high level of academic teaching available at either Elsinby Castle or later at Maddleskirk College. I was unsure whether Charles could compete with some of the extremely bright children who'd be his competitors even in the primary school class. He was a shy and very quiet lad while many of his classmates were the sons of tutors and staff at Maddleskirk College. Before becoming parents and teachers, they had all been through the best universities and colleges, they had travelled the world and were widely read. Another factor against Charles was that they spoke with the right accent, not English with a strong Yorkshire flavour like my family and me. I must admit I worried whether he would be accepted by the posh kids—or even by the staff. There was a lot to consider and the welfare of our son was of paramount importance. I knew that children could be very cruel to someone who did not fit their vision of the world or match their social class or who was different in some way. And the son of a village bobby was quite different, if only because his dad was a copper. The basic fact was that Charles would not have an easy time at any secondary school, whether or not he won a scholarship . . . police officers' children did get teased or worse . . . bullying was common in many schools even if it was done without the knowledge of the staff.

Because everything was suddenly so riddled with doubt, we decided neither to tell the children nor indeed anyone else about the beat closure at this stage, neither would I reveal my impending move from Aidensfield until I had been interviewed by the chief constable. Hopefully, that meeting would clarify my very uncertain future.

Next morning, my first task was to interview Claude Jeremiah Greengrass about the alleged offence of his cruelty to a dog but when I arrived at his scruffy smallholding shortly after ten o'clock, there was no sign of him. His truck was not parked outside the house either, but after a quick search, I found no sign of a 'dog cart' or even a dog. I must be sure to tell Mrs Potiphar otherwise she'd be ringing every day . . .

Over the next few days, which included the weekend, I hunted the elusive Claude Greengrass without locating him or his 'dog cart' either at his home or in the lanes around Aidensfield. So where had he gone? And what was he up to?

I did keep Mrs Potiphar informed, asking that she notify me if she spotted him anywhere. During those tours, I gave a lot of thought to what I regarded as a personal predicament.

Somehow, to achieve my unlikely dreams of having the best education for my family—and I did want a settled education for them in addition to a settled home life—I had to find my way through the quagmire of police regulations, procedures and policies, and also cope with the dictates of some very senior officers. Fortunately during those few days, my beat was peaceful with no reported crimes, accidents or incidents—thus providing yet more ammunition for Headquarters in their bid to close it!

I made a point of patrolling the most remote parts of my beat where I could park the mini-van and sit quietly in an attempt to assess my situation while also trying to work out some kind of strategy for my unknown future. I felt like a juggler keeping several balls in the air at the same time, but the worst thing was that I was not in command of my own family's destiny, nor even my own. I did not own a house; I had no property of my own and my fate was in the hands of the police service. I felt rather trapped, I must admit.

One fact was significant, I felt. It was stated in police regulations that the service had to supply houses for its members or alternatively pay an allowance in lieu. There is no doubt that living in a rent-and-rate free police house had lots of advantages to a young, hard-up family but, as I had often thought to myself, if I was killed on duty or seriously injured to the extent of having to leave the service, then I and my family would have nowhere to live. If I was killed, whether on duty or not, my widow and family would not be allowed to remain permanently in police accommodation.

In a county force, police houses were needed for staff and to facilitate police duty, but I realized that policemen who retired needed other homes because they were no longer permitted to live in police houses. A police house, even if it was rent-free during one's years of service, was therefore a stumbling block. I became determined to find a legitimate way of securing my own home within the provision of police regulations and procedures—it was a vital factor to consider and the time was right now.

It helped to know that some officers were permitted to occupy and purchase their own houses. Those serving in city and borough forces could buy their own homes because they did not have to perform their duties beyond the boundaries of their own rather compact force area. Within the much larger area of a county, those owning their homes were usually fairly senior officers or sometimes lower ranks who could expect to remain at their current posts for several years. Even so, the rules said they must transfer when ordered to, even if it meant selling or renting their own house and moving into police property. Most young officers in the service would not be expected to tie themselves to their own property—it would defeat the purpose of police regulations and it would restrict the promotion opportunities of an officer. But even as I was contemplating all this, change was in the air.

Perhaps I was fortunate because, in the 1960s, more and more officers, of all ranks and ages in county forces, were applying to their Chief Constables for permission to purchase their own homes. In many cases, this permission was granted but always with the proviso that if they were transferred to another post in a different part of the county they would have to leave or even sell their house—and move back into police-owned property if necessary. In such cases, renting their house to someone else was always an option if they did not want to sell it but transfers also affected working wives and the schooling of children. Having a settled home life was becoming more important to police officers in the shires. There was also a financial factor for the Force to consider—if officers occupied their own homes, it would reduce police expenditure on maintaining police houses, paying for repairs and meeting the costs of the rates. In short, it would be more cost effective for police forces if their officers lived in their own homes because it would reduce the financial drain on the Home Office and local authorities. Both the Home Office and the police service were coming around to that idea, and there was no statutory reason why a police officer should not travel to his place of work like any other citizen.

With all this in mind, I felt the time was right for me to float my own ideas. Policemen serving on rural beats, however, could not buy the police house in which they lived—it was officially a police station with an office attached and was considered part of the over-all job of being a rural constable. It was always needed for the constable, although it could be sold if the beat was closed. So would that apply to Aidensfield police house when I left? Indeed, when Aidensfield beat closed, would I be able to buy that house? I began to wonder whether I could find the means—and a sound reason—for buying a house in Aidensfield or nearby while serving elsewhere within commuting distance of any new posting.

Happily, there was another important asset for a police officer buying his or her own house. This was based on regulations that stipulated the police service was obliged to accommodate its officers free of charge in police-owned or police-rented accommodation. If for any reason that was not possible or desirable, officers could live in private rented accommodation and might qualify for a rent allowance that could be extended to officers buying their own homes. This constituted a wonderful means of getting significant help with the payment of a mortgage. But such a diversion from the norm required the chief constable's written consent.

For all sorts of reasons, therefore, owning one's own house made a lot of sense quite apart from the fact that it was a superb investment. As much as Mary and I liked Aidensfield, I decided I did not really want to buy the disused police house—to live there would always put me at risk of being called out to incidents or being knocked up in the middle of the night by people needing a police officer. People would think I was still the village bobby even if I was working at a distant police station. And, of course, I would still be a policeman with all the responsibilities of the office which meant I should not refuse to turn out! So living in or buying the old police house was not an option I would consider. In any case, it was rapidly becoming too small for my family of four growing children.

What about other houses for sale in Aidensfield and district? I'd need a house very quickly but one bonus was that I did not have a house to sell—I would be a first-time buyer so there would be no chain of purchasers. Nonetheless, I would have to secure the chief constable's permission to buy my own house, wherever it was. That could be difficult or even impossible for one so very young in service.

As I pondered my options, I knew that to live near Aidensfield, albeit in a different village, had lots of appeal.

I would be a normal resident commuting to work like other people. My children would continue with their local schooling, my wife would retain all her friends and contacts, she would be able to obtain work if necessary and we would possess a property that would increase in value as the years passed by. Hopefully, my mortgage would be paid before I retired—then I'd be living in a free house! Such an arrangement would make complete sense even if I did not win promotion and I was sure we could find a suitable property in the area. And, of course, as a family, we would have that important assurance of security for the future. Such a lot depended upon what the chief constable told me on Monday.

On the Sunday night, Mrs Potiphar rang again to say she had seen Greengrass and his 'dog cart' along the lane between Elsinby and Ploatby, and so I updated her about my fruitless hunt for the elusive old rogue.

'Perhaps tomorrow, PC Rhea?' she spoke sharply. 'I do get the impression you are not taking this matter very seriously . . .'

'Tomorrow, Mrs Potiphar, I have to attend Police Headquarters at Northallerton for a meeting with the chief constable. I do not know what time I shall return. But rest assured I will deal with the matter as soon as is feasible.'

'I should think you will!' she snapped and slammed down the receiver.

That Sunday night once the children were in bed, we settled down to count our meagre savings and to look at house prices in the villages; in our picturesque part of Yorkshire they were expensive—around £2,500 to £3,250 for a nice three bed-roomed semi-detached house and between £5,000 and £6,000 for a four or five bed-roomed detached property with a garden. What I needed was a good bank manager, a friendly building society and a large slice of good luck. And on top of all that, I must find a suitable property!

By Monday morning I had persuaded myself that whatever the outcome of my meeting with the chief constable, I would actively pursue the option of buying a house because it would provide the security I felt I lacked. Before leaving for my important meeting, I kissed the children goodbye as they left for school, giving Charles a special hug to wish him every success in his exam.

He'd insisted he wanted to take the exam because many of his friends from primary school were also sitting it; these pupils were chiefly the sons of teachers or administrative staff at the college. He would be taken to the castle by the school and returned afterwards so I did not have to transport him there. By one of those odd coincidences, he would be starting his exam at 11 a.m., precisely the time I would be suffering my own ordeal in front of the chief constable. It was to be a big day for the menfolk of the Rhea family.

Leaving the police house with a kiss and hug from Mary, and dressed in my best uniform, I drove my mini-van down to Ashfordly Police Station because I had some reports to deliver to the sergeant. Alf Ventress was on office duty and said he would attend to my paper work, then he wished me every success at Headquarters. Clearly, he was curious about the reason for my interview, but I had to tell him I had no idea why I had been summoned to the presence of the great.

'Honestly, Alf, I've no idea.'

'There's a rumour they're closing Aidensfield beat,' he smiled conspiratorially. 'I heard it in the Black Swan, one of the police committee members was discussing it with his pals . . . if it's true, Nick, you ought to get Blaketon to mount some kind of mass objection on behalf of the village. We can do without beats closing, the public rely on us to be there when we're needed. Maybe the Chief wants to discuss it with you?'

'I doubt it, Alf, such things are not generally open to discussion. If it's going to be closed, then that is what will happen, irrespective of what I say.'

I had difficulty assuring him I had absolutely no idea what was going on so far as Aidensfield beat was concerned, but told him I hoped to have more information when I returned from Headquarters.

In the meantime, I suggested that perhaps he and his colleagues in Ashfordly would look out for signs of Greengrass and his 'dog cart'?

'Oh, the inspector's been on about that, Nick. Apparently some woman is making a fuss about it. She's ringing him and has even rung the Superintendent.'

'Well, I'm on the case, Alf, but Greengrass has vanished. I've been to his place and there's no sign of him or a "dog cart".'

'Maybe that's what the chief constable wants to discuss with you? That woman is very persistent.'

'Just keep an eye on the quiet lanes around here, Alf. We need to find out what Greengrass is up to. Now I must go and see what the Chief wants.'

And so I departed from Ashfordly Police Station for the journey of about an hour. I made sure I was smart—my hair had been trimmed and washed, my boots were shining like a guardsman's, my trousers had creases like knife-edges and there wasn't a hint of dandruff on my tunic. And I had polished the peak of my cap.

I knew my way around Police Headquarters having worked there before my posting to Aidensfield and indeed knew most of the staff. For that reason, I was probably more relaxed than those poor souls who had never been within these mighty portals. After parking the mini-van in the visitors' car park, I made my way to the office of the chief constable's secretary. Before going into her office, I popped into the Gents where I could check my appearance in the mirror and put myself at ease. At ten minutes to eleven, I rapped on the secretary's door and poked my head into her office. Her name was Jean.

'Hi, Jean, it's Nick Rhea, I've an appointment with the Chief at eleven.'

'Hello, Nick. Good to see you back here. Doesn't time fly! It's hardly any time since you were part of our staff. If you'd like to take a seat in the waiting room, I'll tell the Chief you've arrived and he'll call you when he's ready.'

Being the chief constable's waiting room, there was a coffee percolator and a fresh brew so I helped myself, albeit being careful not to spill any down my smart uniform. As I sipped, I felt remarkably at ease—after all, I had met the Chief many times when I'd worked here so he was no stranger to me. I was aware of one risk however—sometimes, new or inexperienced cleaners polished the floor beneath the rug which lay directly in front of the Chief's desk. I remembered one nervous officer who marched into the room, stamped his feet upon the rug to come briskly to attention like a guardsman at Buckingham Palace and promptly skidded as the rug slid forward. Unable to stop himself, he became a one-legged passenger on a low flying carpet. He finished up lying on his back under the chief constable's huge desk with the rug wrapped all around him. I was determined not to let that happen to me.

'He's ready for you,' Jean arrived with a smile. 'You know the routine. March in, come to a halt in front of his desk and salute him. Then sit down on the chair provided and put your cap on your lap with your hands on top—and don't fiddle with your fingers or anything else. It's a sign of nervousness.'

'Thanks Jean.' I appreciated her friendly advice and smiled my appreciation as she paused to allow her words to register with me.

Then she continued, 'And when the interview is over, stand up, put your cap on, salute him again and march smartly out of the room.'

She opened the huge ornate door and I strode forward, saw the chair and the rug, marched towards them, slung up a fine salute and settled on the chair with my cap on my lap.

'Ah, Rhea,' the chief constable welcomed me with a warm and genuine smile. 'Good to see you again. Like old times, eh? You coming to my office for all sorts of important reasons.'

He always called police officers by their surname and never by their rank.

'It's a change from rural Aidensfield, sir.'

'I'm sure it is. Now, I'll come straight to the point because I know you'll be wondering why I have called you here for this chat. I am sure you're aware of the developments affecting your beat at Aidensfield?'

'Yes, sir. I have been told. I must say I'm sorry—and surprised—it's going to close.'

'Aren't we all? That's the price of progress, Rhea, the result of more than a little interference from our political masters. It's happening all over the country, beats and even sections and divisions are being amalgamated. We're having to police larger areas with fewer officers and less money, but I can understand your sorrow at leaving such a wonderful place. I am aware of your record there, by the way, both official and unofficial—I have many old friends who live close to Aidensfield and all report well of you and your family. That kind of unofficial feedback gives me immense pleasure, Rhea, far better than relying on formal reports from supervisory officers. Much more realistic and invariably reliable.'

'Thank you sir.'

'However, we're not here to talk about Aidensfield, we're here to talk about you and I must say I am very interested in your writing capabilities—I often see your work in magazines and periodicals, legal journals included. We get a wide selection here as you know, as well as local papers and periodicals, and I try to read them all.'

'It's a very pleasant hobby, sir.' I hoped he wasn't going to stop me writing!

'I am sure it is. Now, as a chief constable, I have to keep abreast of national and local affairs and I know you do the occasional broadcast on North Region BBC radio programmes.'

'It enables me to learn all manner of useful information as I go along even if it is only a hobby.' I said that because, sometime earlier, I'd had to obtain his written permission to accept payment for my contributions.

'Well, the Force can bask in your reflected glory and I know you will always be discreet so far as confidentiality is concerned. That is most important and I wish you well. But let me tell you this. I was staying with a friend a couple of weekends ago. He owns a modest estate on the western edge of the moors. Nice chap, very capable and a good friend. We were having breakfast and we listening to The Northern Farmer—he always listens to the programme. And you came on, Rhea. A piece about the law and practice relating to sheep worrying.'

'Yes, sir, I wrote it and recorded it.'

At this point, I began to think I was in trouble of some kind. Had I made a serious mistake in my interpretation of the law, or was I breaking one or other of police regulations by broadcasting in that way? But I could not deny making that broadcast so should I have obtained his prior permission?

'It was very well done if I may say so. You made it sound interesting. You've clearly got a knack for putting over dry legal pieces and making them worth listening to, even if you have no legal qualifications. And I haven't forgotten that you won second prize in the Queen's annual Police Gold Medal Essay competition recently.'

'Oh, well, thank you, sir.' I was sure he hadn't summoned me to Police Headquarters merely to congratulate me on a very minor broadcast or my essay.

'I've been looking at your records. I see that at the initial training school, you developed an aptitude for learning and understanding criminal law. You came top of your course, as I well remember.'

'It was the first time I'd come top in anything!' I tried to make light of this. 'So I've kept up my interest in criminal law . . . writing about it enables to me explore those laws that affect particular sections of the general public—say farmers, pub landlords, coin collectors, fishermen, car owners or whatever—and it means I can write explanatory pieces on subjects that closely affect them.'

'So could you do the same for police officers? Could you explain the complexities of criminal law and police procedure in a manner that seasoned police officers could understand or even enjoy?'

'I'm sure I could, sir. I've written such articles for *Police Review*. Teaching police officers would be a case of matching the law to whatever they are likely to deal with in the street, giving real examples of how to make use of the legislation. I believe that knowledge of the law is vital for a police officer patrolling the beat.'

'I couldn't agree more, but I must say that some are not very *au fait* with our laws.'

'It's not easy. They have to think on their feet and act with speed, confidence and accuracy in any given situation—they've no law books on hand to help them. So yes, I'm sure I could explain things without being too heavy and dry.'

'I'm pleased to hear your response, Rhea. Which brings me to the point of this meeting.'

He paused but I knew better than interrupt.

He continued. 'In a week or two, we shall need a new sergeant instructor in criminal law and police procedure; the vacancy will be at our Force Training School. I'm sure you know Solberge very well.'

I did know it well. I'd been there on refresher courses. It was a fine country house in its own grounds on a hilltop just outside Northallerton. Called Solberge Hall which means Sunny Hill, it accommodated residential courses of three-weeks duration for police officers from all over the north-east of England, including the British Transport Commission police. It was quite separate from the Home Office Police

Training Centre which was just a mile away at Newby Wiske Hall—that dealt with raw recruits while Solberge accommodated seasoned and experienced officers up to and including the rank of inspector who were attending refresher courses. An extra dimension was that a sergeant from Solberge Hall also visited out-stations around the county to update officers on new legislation and to assist those studying for promotion examinations. In that case, a car allowance was payable.

I could hardly believe what I was hearing . . . me a law instructor? Promoted to Sergeant . . . is that what he was leading to?

'Yes, sir,' I said. 'I've always enjoyed Solberge courses.'

'Good. Well, as you know, there's a small but dedicated staff, Rhea. A commandant who is a chief inspector by rank, two sergeants and a constable tutor. The constable is a superb lecturer who incredibly has never passed his promotion exams so we can't promote him. One of the sergeants will be retiring at the end of June and I would like you to take his place with effect from July 1st.'

'Good grief, sir!' was all I could think of saying. 'Me? Teaching all those experienced police officers?'

'They might be very experienced and capable on the streets, Rhea, but they do need to be updated regularly with changes in the law, and reminded about existing legislation, not to mention new procedures that may be imposed either by the Home Office or at a more local level. Candidates meet officers from other police forces throughout the north on these courses, which is also beneficial because it widens one's perspective of the job while establishing contacts that may be useful in the future. Now, the post does mean promotion to sergeant and so I have to ask you if you will accept it, with all the responsibilities it entails?'

'Well, yes sir, of course. With great pleasure.' I could hardly believe my ears.

'That is what I hoped you would say. Well, congratulations. I am convinced you are the right man for the job.' At that point, he stood up, extended his hand for me to shake, and smiled his pleasure. I did likewise and did not quite know what to say or do next, but he sat down, so I did likewise. He continued. 'Now, Rhea, there is a small problem on which I need your co-operation. You have a large family?'

'Four children, sir. It's a small family by Aidensfield standards. At our Catholic primary school, our family was the smallest with only four—there was a family of thirteen, a twelve, a ten, several nines and eights, a seven or a few sixes . . .'

'That a good Catholic village for you!' he grinned. 'However, standard police houses aren't really built for families with four or more children. The only vacant ones at the moment are two semi-detached properties in Northallerton, both with three bedrooms. But the third bedroom is little more than a boxroom—far too tiny for a bed, but probably suitable for a cot. With a fast-growing family, you'd be very cramped for space . . .'

This was my cue. I couldn't let this one pass by!

'Could I buy a house, sir?'

'You can afford to do that?' the surprise was evident on his face.

'No more than any other police officer, I'd have to get a mortgage, but I have some savings. And there is a reason for the question, sir.'

Perhaps being very presumptuous, I told him about Charles and the exam he had already passed, and the one he was taking at that very moment.

'You mean that your son might qualify to attend one of the country's finest public schools?'

'Yes, sir, possibly on a scholarship, provided he does well in today's exam. He has already passed the preliminary test.'

'Good grief, man, you can't miss an opportunity like this. So why does buying a house become so important?'

'The scholarships are only for day-boys, sir; in fact, any other vacancies would also be for day-boys only. So we'd have to live in the vicinity of the school.'

'Hmm, well, this is rather unusual but times are changing within the police service. And about time too!'

He paused and I could see him pondering my dilemma.

'You could be breaking new ground, Rhea, but we do need to get away from our rigid adherence to rules and regulations and I do like my officers to consider their own futures and be responsible for themselves. Rules and regulations can be flexible when one studies them, as I am sure you know. I see no reason why you shouldn't buy a house as you suggest—or even rent one—and commute to work like anyone else; millions of other people do it. And working at Solberge means you'll get your main meal of the day free of charge because you will be eating with the students, and if the roads are covered in snow, there'll always be a bed for the night. Look, this is not a decision I can make right here and now. Wait until your son's results are known and if he passes and is offered a scholarship, ring my secretary and she will alert me. Then you must submit a written request to be allowed to buy your own house—or rent one privately—for the reasons you have described, and I will approve it. It will be your responsibility to get to work every day on time in spite of breakdowns, hold-ups, punctures and other problems, not to mention our winter weather, but let's be honest, people in other jobs and professions manage to do so, so why shouldn't a capable police officer do likewise? So it all rests upon the narrow shoulders of your little son, eh?'

'It does indeed, sir, but whatever happens I would like to take the Solberge promotion.'

'And so you shall. Now I suggest you go home, speak to your wife and start looking at houses for sale. If it does take a long time to find one, I am sure we could let you remain in Aidensfield Police House for a few weeks until you find a suitable property of your own, but don't outstay your welcome . . . this is an unofficial concession.'

'I won't abuse it, sir.'

'I know you won't. I trust you. Well, off you go, you've a lot to think about and if I were you, I'd ring the Commandant at Solberge and get him to send you a typical programme for one of the courses along with a file of lecture notes. Then you can start swotting up the laws and preparing your own lectures long before you're thrown in at the proverbial deep end as a new tutor.'

'Thank you, sir. I will.'

'I wish you every success in your endeavours. I am sure you know that promotion is not a reward for past work, but an investment in what you can do for the future benefit of the Force.'

'Yes, sir, I understand that. And thank you most sincerely.'

'Good, and if all your plans fail, then you can live in a police house at Northallerton, that is always an option even if it will be rather cramped until you find somewhere else,' and he stood up again to indicate that the interview was over and leaned over to shake my hand once more. I stood up, shook his hand, replaced my cap, saluted and left his office after thanking him again.

Now I had lots to tell Mary. But as I drove home with my exciting news, I wondered whether I should write an article about the law relating to 'dog-carts' but at the same time I could hardly wait to see how Charles had fared with his own special test.

And where on earth had Greengrass got to?

CHAPTER 3

The outward journey to Police Headquarters had only taken an hour or so as fortunately I had not encountered any incident that required my attention en route. The return journey took around the same time and so, including my interview, the entire trip had taken about two and a half hours. It meant there remained a large proportion of my eight-hour patrol still to complete. Itching to tell Mary my news I drove straight home to Aidensfield because I was due for a refreshment break of forty-five minutes. When I parked in my drive shortly before 1 p.m., I radioed Alf Ventress at Ashfordly Police Station and booked myself off duty at Aidensfield Police House for refreshments.

'Message received and understood,' responded Alf, knowing it was against regulations and he could not use the police wavelength for gossip and chit-chat. He'd be dying to know why I had been summoned to Headquarters. 'And by the way, we've had a report from a man in Crampton who said Greengrass was seen heading through the village early this morning with his dog cart. He's not been seen since. The chap who rang in thought it was drawn by a pair of huskies. Mush, mush! Over and out.'

I decided not to tell him my news just yet because Mary must be first, even if there were ways of circumventing the regulations. I knew one constable in a city whose wife was in the maternity hospital with their child due while he was on patrol. Long before personal radio sets were invented, the police station received news of the birth and passed it to the proud dad on his beat in this way—'Control to Yankee 67' (his shoulder number). 'Control to Yankee 67. Bicycle delivered, pump attached.' He knew that his son had been born.

In another instance, I heard a Control Room sergeant using the police radio to contact a constable on the beat with this coded message, 'Control to Yankee 36. H and C 2 please. H and C 2.'

'What's that mean?' I asked in my youthful ignorance.

'It means the sergeant is ordering supper for the Control Room staff—haddock and chips twice,' was the reply.

I knew of no code to inform Alf of my news, but I would tell Alf and the others in due course. I might even pop into Ashfordly Police Station in the afternoon. I had no idea where the sergeant or inspector had gone but I thought I might risk stretching my refreshment break by a few minutes in view of the remarkable change to my fortunes—not that a sergeant's pay was much greater than a senior constable's. Certainly it would not enable me to pay school fees! But Mary would be waiting for my news, whatever it was.

Over a quiet lunch while the children were at school, I could pass my good news to her. She was waiting when I returned—she'd worked out from my 11 a.m. interview (and the fact I hadn't taken sandwiches and there was no canteen in Police HQ) that I would probably come home for lunch. She had even set the table in the dining room. It looked lovely with our best crockery, glassware and a vase of flowers, far smarter than the kitchen. And she had removed all my writing paraphernalia from the table. Even though I should not normally drink while on duty, I felt a single glass of white wine would be in order today—after all, we were celebrating and I'd noticed she had placed a bottle in the fridge. There were times I felt that female intuition was quite remarkable! Rather than risk driving my police van immediately after the wine, I could undertake a foot patrol in the village but one or two small glasses would not make me unfit to drive.

Upon seeing the table so nicely set, however, I wondered whether she had really sensed I would be celebrating or was it to help drown my sorrows? Whatever her reason, it was a thoughtful gesture and so typical—we'd finish off the remainder of the wine tonight! With the assistance of my Ashfordly colleagues, I might even be able to take off my boots and replace them with slippers! And if Mrs Potiphar rang tonight, I would not answer the phone; she could discuss Greengrass's 'dog cart' with one of the Ashfordly team—but was he really using huskies? I tried not to be concerned at this juncture and explained to Mary that I would provide her with details of my interview once we had settled down to eat—it was no good trying to chat while she was preparing lunch.

'So,' she had served a plate of warm chicken nuggets with fresh salad from a large bowl, an ideal light lunch. 'What have you got to tell me?'

In response, I reached for the bottle of wine and poured two glasses. I raised mine, she raised hers and I said, 'It's a celebration, Mary. I've been promoted to sergeant as from 1 July.'

'Oh, Nick . . . I guessed it must be something like that because you were going to see the chief constable. I knew you wouldn't be in any kind of trouble . . . I'm so pleased for you, I really am. I always knew you would be successful . . . cheers.'

We clicked our glasses in the traditional toasting gesture then she leaned over and kissed me before we settled down to our meal.

'So where will you be posted now that you are to be a sergeant?' was her first and entirely understandable question, her face suddenly showing more than a hint of concern. Most new sergeants were posted to busy town beats to gain the required experience.

'Solberge Hall,' I smiled. 'The Force Training School. It'll mean weekends off and regular hours, and I'll get my main daily meals because I shall be eating with the students. It means I'll be on duty at meal time, a sort of supervisory role. There's also a car allowance because I'll be travelling around the Force area to organize refresher courses and some probationer training. It's a dream job, Mary. Right up my street.'

She didn't seem too pleased at this point; I could sense she was not sharing my enthusiasm because her pretty face was frowning as she said, 'But that's near Northallerton, isn't it? Does it mean we'll have to live in Northallerton? In a police house?'

'Not necessarily,' and I now played my trump card. 'And here's another stroke of luck. The Chief agrees that modern police houses with two medium-sized bedrooms and a third, little bigger than a boxroom are not suitable for a family of four growing children. At the moment, though, he has no larger police houses to offer. I leapt in straight away to ask if I could buy a house and I stressed the reason—saying we'd like to continue living in this area.'

'You didn't ask him that, surely? What a nerve! Didn't that put the Chief into some kind of predicament? Just as he was offering you promotion, you decide to ask for special favours! Nick, you didn't to that, surely? It's a wonder he didn't turn you down!'

'It wasn't like that at all!'

'So what really happened?' there was a frown on her pretty face.

'He said yes! Or rather, he said he would approve my application if and when I submitted it in writing through the usual channels. I can imagine some eyebrows being raised at Divisional and at Sub-Division level, but that doesn't worry me.'

'I still think you had a nerve to ask him that! And at that particular time.'

'The Chief said things were changing, the police service is becoming more accommodating to the needs of its staff. So there we are, our timing was just right so I will phrase the application to make sure it goes direct to the chief constable without some trumped-up senior officer refusing me permission by failing to pass on my application. But . . .' and I paused in my narrative.

'I thought there'd be a catch . . .'

'There isn't, not really. If we get our own home there will be the usual condition that I must agree to serve anywhere within the county, moving house if necessary, but it all depends on the result of Charles's exam.'

'Oh dear . . .'

'The Chief was quite taken with the idea of a policeman's son going to Elsinby Castle Prep School and then on to Maddleskirk College, and he said we shouldn't miss such a wonderful opportunity.'

'So it all depends on little Charles? I wonder how he's got on today,' Mary was thinking aloud. 'Poor little chap, such a trial for a seven-year-old . . .'

'Whatever happens, we mustn't let him know that the purchase of a house depends on his entrance exam result!' I said. 'If he fails, the Chief will still let me buy a house due to the size of our family, but it might not be where we want it. It may have to be close to the training school. That's the problem. But I shall do my best to impress on the Chief that really the Aidensfield area is very suitable—driving a distance to work is no problem and there are lots of stations to which I can commute when I complete my posting to Solberge. I can work at Eltering, Ashfordly, Malton, Thirsk, Pickering. It shouldn't hinder my progress up the promotion ladder.'

'There are times, Nick Rhea, when I think that if you fell into a midden you'd still come up smelling of roses!'

'That's because I'm alert enough to take advantage of prevailing situations. So now, Mary, we have a very important and rather urgent task ahead. I have to find Greengrass who is apparently using huskies to haul a "dog cart", which upsets Mrs Potiphar, and then we—I mean we—have to find a suitable house within the next six weeks or so. Then we must secure the approval of our bank manager and a building society. They might take some persuading that my idea is sensible and practical. Fortunately, we don't have a house to sell which puts us in a position of some strength but before I leave here I've got to swot up on my legal knowledge so I can lecture to serving and widely experienced police officers when I take up my new job. And finally, I have to keep this beat running efficiently until I leave, making sure I tie up the proverbial loose ends before I finish at Aidensfield.'

'You're in for a busy time, then?'

'*We're* in for a busy time. A lot is going to happen in the next few weeks, Mary. Anyway, that's my day in a nutshell. How about yours?'

'I suppose I've been hanging around waiting for my two men to come with their news! One has arrived with good news, but we won't hear from Charles until he comes in after school.'

'Then I'll try and sneak home early—I can always make the excuse my radio isn't working properly and that I want to use the phone in my office! Meanwhile, I think I'll have another glass of wine and then I'll ring the office to tell Alf I'm going to do a brief foot patrol of Aidensfield, checking dog licences and looking for Greengrass and his "dog cart". I can find plenty of reasons for not taking the van out and it's a fact that the radio doesn't work in some areas of my beat.'

'What if it's an emergency . . . ?'

'Alf will cope, there are plenty of other patrols on duty. I don't have to turn out for minor matters, and if it's really serious Alf and his team will attend.'

'I don't want you to get caught drinking on duty.'

'Two small glasses of white wine won't make me unfit to drive. I want a quiet evening with you—so here's to us,' and we raised our glasses a second time. I had decided not to drive anywhere just yet, not because I'd drunk two small glasses of wine, but because I really wanted to walk slowly along

Aidensfield's main street in my uniform at this emotional moment. I wasn't particularly concerned about Greengrass and his "dog cart"—there was plenty of time for me to trace him. In any case, I would soon have to inform the people living on my beat about my impending move, and then come to terms with the fact that this was no longer 'my' village.

I continued to find it difficult to imagine this peace-loving community without a resident constable and I hoped the powers-that-be knew what they were doing. It all seemed so short-sighted—old Father Time together with a rising crime rate would surely emphasize the unrealistic nature of this political decisions.

In that way I contrived to be at home with the rest of the family when Charles returned with his news. We were all keen to find out what had transpired at Elsinby Castle but, like most seven-year-olds, he wasn't very communicative. All he said was. 'It was all right.'

'Did you do well?' I pressed.

'I don't know, I haven't got my marks yet.'

'Were there many other boys taking the exam?' asked Mary.

'Oh yes, sixty or seventy, from all over England, Wales and Scotland. And some from America, Canada and Australia. Most were there because their parents had applied for them to be boarders, they weren't from local schools like our group was. If we passed, we'd be the only day-boys there, the others would all be boarders. We filled the Great Chamber with our desks . . . it went on for a long time. The monks looked after us and we had our lunches there.'

'A big turn-out then. And were there several tests?'

'Yes, maths, English, geography and history combined, then general knowledge. Half an hour for each paper, Dad. Two before lunch—they gave us lunch there. With all the other boys . . . there's lots of them in the school, it's much bigger than ours, then there were two tests after lunch. Then those from Aidensfield school were taken back in the minibus while the other boys went home with their parents.'

'So when will you get to know the result?'

'They said it would not be before Friday next week. They'll send a letter to our schools, addressed to you, and I'll have to bring it home.'

'So all we can do is wait, Charles, but meanwhile well done. We're proud of you—to get yourself in the final selection of seventy or whatever from all over the country is a massive achievement. So it's fingers crossed until we get that letter!'

I explained to my family that I still had an hour or so to fulfil before my daytime patrol officially ended and, now confident I was not unfit to drive a motor vehicle due to alcohol (this was before the breath test was introduced), headed for Ashfordly Police Station to pass the news to my colleagues. The sergeant was at a sub-divisional meeting in Eltering Police Station and the town constables were out on patrol but as always, Alf Ventress was staffing the counter.

'Well, hello Nick. We've all been wondering what's happened, you being called up to the Star Chamber at Northallerton. Not in bother, are you?'

'No, nothing like that, Alf. I'm moving—those rumours you heard about the closure of Aidensfield beat were correct. It shuts down at the end of June. The work will be divided between remaining beats and the team here at Ashfordly, but the house is going to be sold. I don't know the full details yet.'

'That's a tragedy, it really is. So what's happening to you? Are you coming here to join us here, as a beatman in Ashfordly? We could always do with an extra hand or two, especially if Greengrass continues to tour the area with his "dog cart".'

'Sorry, no, Alf. I'm being transferred to Solberge Hall.'

'Really? The training school? I've never seen you as an academic type, a boffin or professor or whatever they're called. How do you feel about that?'

'I'm very pleased,' I spoke the truth. 'It's not training recruits as I'm sure you know, it's for refreshing more seasoned police officers, those with a lot of service under their belts, updating them with changes in the law and brushing up their knowledge of existing laws. There will be probationers to teach as well, and perhaps those on courses who are studying for promotion exams. I'll enjoy that.'

'Does that mean you'll be promoted then?'

'Yes, Alf. I'll be a sergeant.'

'Good grief, we'll all have to watch our p's and q's then! But congratulations, and I mean it, Nick. It's always pleasing to see young lads getting on in the world.'

'You never tried for promotion, did you?'

'No, I was OK with exams, but I've never wanted the responsibility that goes with rank. I'm happiest doing what I'm doing now. My job here fits me like a cosy old sweater. So when does all this happen to you?'

'The end of June,' I said. 'I'll be a sergeant with effect from July 1.'

'Great news and congratulations again. So where will you be living?'

'I don't know yet, that's got to the sorted out, especially with my having a large family.' I didn't feel inclined to mention the possibility of a house purchase at that early state. After all, things might go wrong. 'I think they're considering police houses in Northallerton, they've a few empty ones there.'

'Well, I don't know what to say except we'll miss you, but very well done. The first step on the promotion ladder—and the most important. Making sergeant is a vital step, Nick. They say it gets easier after that!'

'And I hope the next step doesn't take so long!'

'It rarely does. You won't forget us, will you? Us ordinary rankers and old codgers out here in the sticks?'

'No, of course not,' and I clapped him on the shoulder. 'Just you try and keep me away from Aidensfield and Ashfordly!'

'Oh, I don't know about that. Once you get mixing with the top brass from Headquarters, you'll forget about us *hoi polloi* and ordinary mortals back here in your old stamping ground.'

'How could I ever forget you and the others, Alf?'

And then the telephone rang. Alf answered it.

'Ashfordly Police, PC Ventress.'

As the caller began to deliver his message, Alf waved at me to remain in the office. I was edging towards the door because it was almost my knocking off time.

He began to write on a piece of paper, saying,

'Yes, I understand. Fine. Yes, got that . . . all right, sir. We'll have someone there in about five minutes. You be sure to remain there until our officer arrives.' And he put down the phone.

'A problem, Alf?'

'Nowt serious, Nick, and sorry to land you with this just as you were going to knock off. It's a two-car collision between Briggsby and Aidensfield, that's on your patch. No injuries, just a couple of badly dented cars and probably a bruised ego or two plus a bit of a hold up with traffic. Shouldn't take much sorting out.'

'All right, Alf, it's on my way home, I'll deal with it. Can you ring Mary and say I'll be late in? Not more than an hour late, I hope.'

'Will do, Nick.'

And so it was back to normal police work as I motored out of Ashfordly en route to yet another routine traffic accident.

* * *

In the days that followed, I called at the Greengrass Farm every day but there was no sign of its resident rogue. It was almost as if the house had been abandoned. There were no vehicles outside and certainly no huskies nor "dog-carts". I kept Mrs Potiphar informed and she was surprised to discover the dogs might be huskies.

'They're trained to haul sleds and carts,' I told her. 'For that reason, I can't see that it is cruel for them to haul a cart

45

on a road. Their instinct is to haul sleds, often with very heavy loads.'

'The law is the law, Mr Rhea, it is illegal for them to do so on our roads,' Mrs Potiphar was a tall angular woman with a large nose, down which she looked upon lesser mortals. 'And as the local RSPCA representative, I am asking you to take the necessary action to prosecute Mr Greengrass.'

'I haven't found him yet, although we have had several sightings.'

'This is highly unsatisfactory, Mr Rhea, this man is getting away with murder.'

'Hardly murder, Mrs Potiphar but I—and my colleagues— are keeping our eyes open for the travelling Mr Greengrass. We are just as curious as you—'

'I am not curious, Mr Rhea. I am trying to enforce the law.'

We parted with an air of mutual distrust.

My priority was to find a suitable house. Fortunately my routine patrolling by day and by night took me into all the villages and hamlets on my patch. But there was a singular lack of suitable houses—I found a huge farmhouse with a hundred and forty acres, but it was too much money and besides, I didn't want such a large amount of land. A small lawn and a patch of garden would suit us fine. Dotted around my beat, however, were lots of small cottages, these often being one or two bedroom properties being disposed of by local estate owners as they found themselves having to recruit fewer staff which in turn reduced the need for estate-owned accommodation.

As I toured the villages with repeated visits to the Greengrass smallholding and enquiries about his movements, Mary also went about her daily routine either in Aidensfield or Ashfordly. When visiting friends she made lots of enquiries about houses that might be for sale in the district. And, like me, she found none. Not even the estate agents had any suitable properties on their books—avidly we scanned all the local papers hoping to find a suitable house, but failed. But all that was within the first few days of receiving my news.

Then Charles came home with the all-important envelope. He had resisted the desire to open it but passed it to Mary who also held it unopened until I returned at tea-time. She gave it to me as we all sat around the tea-table, about to start our meal with the girls being just as interested as we were.

'I think Charles should open it,' and I handed it to him.

We sat and watched as he tore open the large white envelope to extract an official-looking document. It was on the letter-headed paper of Elsinby Castle, complete with crest and motto and he looked down the long screed of writing, reading it in silence. We all sat and waited. Then after an almost insufferable delay, he said, 'I've passed.' Quite spontaneously, the girls applauded.

'Charles, that's absolutely wonderful . . . so can we see the letter?'

''Course you can but it just says I've passed.'

He passed it to me and I read it carefully.

'It doesn't just say you've passed, Charles. You're in the top five, you've beaten almost everyone else from here and overseas and you got 92%. Now I call that brilliant, absolutely brilliant. And this letter is offering you a scholarship to Elsinby Castle, starting with the next autumn term. This September. And continuing until you qualify for the upper school. How about that? Do you really want to go there?'

'Yes,' he said calmly as the girls cheered his decision. 'It would be nice to go. I'd like it there but I hope some of my friends from school go as well.'

'Can we go too?' asked Elizabeth.

'It's only for boys,' and Charles spoke with a surprising air of finality.

'I'm sure some of your friends will have qualified even if they haven't won a scholarship,' I told him. 'Well, this calls for a celebration. Now, my weekly rest days fall this coming weekend so I think we should have a day out somewhere with a special meal in a nice restaurant . . . any ideas?'

'Scarborough, Whitby, Sandsend, Bridlington, Strensford, York . . .' were all shouted out by the family but we settled on Whitby where the sandy beach was convenient for the town, and where there were some mighty good fish and chip shops with restaurant facilities.'

The children liked nothing better than fish-and-chips but I could not forget that I had to swot up my lecture notes and find a house . . . and time was ticking away.

Now that we had Charles's results, I telephoned the Chief's secretary, Jean, as he had suggested, adding that Charles had come fifth out of the entire entry of some seventy boys from around the world and had been awarded a scholarship. I added a reminder about my formal request for permission to buy a house near Aidensfield, and told her it was following in writing. Then I typed it and submitted it 'through the usual channels' which meant it was read by the office staff and everyone else in Ashfordly section office, Eltering sub-division and Malton divisional office before being forwarded to Headquarters.

When they read it, several senior officers telephoned to suggest I was out of my head in making such a bold request— no county police officer could be permitted to buy a house and live such a long way from his place of work. They had to live either on the job or very close to it. 'There's always a first time,' was my standard answer as I stood my ground. 'I want the chief constable himself to make that decision, not someone else and I have already discussed the matter with him in person.'

When the formal note of approval came through, I received a small amount of criticism for being 'well in with those Headquarters lot', 'licking the chief constable's boots' or 'knowing somebody on the police committee'. In response, I used the famous words by Christ quoted in *John 14,13*: 'Whatever you ask in my name, I will do it, that the Father may be glorified in the Son. If you ask anything in my name, I will do it.' Then I grinned, 'So I asked the chief constable and he did it. He's not quite God, but he does rule our lives. It is as simple as that—ask and you shall receive.'

One sergeant went so far as saying, 'But you can't travel to work . . . suppose you break down or get snowed in. It is your duty to parade for duty on time . . .'

'I agree, but there's no law or police regulation that says a police officer can't commute to work like anyone else.'

It was not easy, being a rebellious police officer! But being granted permission to buy a house was a vastly different concept from actually securing one and, of course, paying for it. Now we had to make very determined efforts to find one—and I would have to start overtures with my bank manager and a building society, and all the while, time was ticking away in what seemed an ever-accelerating speed. It was essential for our new home to be close to Elsinby Castle— even within cycling distance for a child—and also within a similar range from Maddleskirk College if Charles excelled himself and eventually won entry to that famous school. Lots of local day-boys cycled to the college and there were short cuts across the valley, although we might have to use the car on occasions.

Taking into consideration all the aspects—and having a home not too remote to make my travelling to work difficult—it meant we should seek one either in one of the villages on my beat, or very close to its boundaries. Somehow, in all the excitement of those times, the problem of raising the necessary money never occurred to me. I had set my heart of achieving something distinctive and ambitious and was heading steadfastly in that direction without any real thoughts as to how I would pay for my plans.

As I patrolled all my villages almost daily, I reckoned I would be first to know if a local house was coming, or had come, onto the market. Finding a suitable one became close to an obsession.

The communities on my beat included: Aidensfield, Elsinby, Seavham, Briggsby, Crampton, Ploatby, Waindale, Rannackdale, Gelderslack, Shelvingby, Lairsbeck, Lower Keld, Thackerston and Stovensby. Some of these were scarcely large enough to be classified a village—scarcely a hamlet, being merely a cluster of houses tucked away in a remote dale or on a hilltop. Not far from my beat were larger villages such as Maddleskirk, Pattington and Falconbridge, and we were all surrounded by a cluster of attractive market towns which included Ashfordly, Eltering, Brantsford, Rammington, Harrowby, Galtreford, Malton, Pickering, Thirsk and Northallerton. Surely I could find a suitable house among that wonderful selection of charming small places? Fortunately, my current job took me around many of these and so I could keep my eyes open for 'For Sale' signs or even 'To Let' if things didn't work out. I did not want to rent a property unless there was no alternative.

With my mind made up and with the approval of my chief constable to support my efforts, I set about planning my new career which, I realized, was actually like being offered a job that was totally different from my existing one. But one essential task was to leave my beat in a good condition. I could not ignore that.

There was the inevitable matter of ensuring that all outstanding reports had been finalized particularly those involving road traffic accidents and offences where a possible court case was pending. In addition I had to ensure that every reported crime had been investigated as far as possible and was complete with an up-to-date report on its progress.

I had to complete all my returns of routine checks of licensed premises, betting shops, farmers' livestock registers, dog licences; all my firearms certificate records had to be up to date and, of course, any defects in the condition of the police house, its office and grounds must also be notified so that any necessary repairs could be effected. I had to ensure that the Beat Report (a loose-leaf collection of facts about the beat, along with details of important personalities, persistent complainers, accident black spots, public houses, post offices, shops and so on) was up to date. It was a veritable goldmine of information about the beat that had been compiled and updated by successive constables. The inventory of the house's official contents had also to be checked, such as the office desk and chair, telephone, map of the district, stationery, the official mini-van and its onboard equipment such as a stretcher, car rug, tape measure, brushes, shovels, emergency lighting and tool kit.

There seemed to be hundreds of small jobs to complete but there were two tasks that had not been resolved. One was to find Greengrass and the second was my footpath. Maybe, for the latter, this was the time to issue a reminder.

It concerned a footpath on Aidensfield Bank. The fact was that there was no footpath beside that road and I thought this steep hill should have a least one formal footpath leading from the village to the summit, a distance of about a third of a mile. There was a small community living at the top of the bank including the police house, six council houses, three farms and four private dwellings, all of which generated people and children. Most were obliged to walk into the village if they wanted to visit the shop, the post office, the telephone kiosk, the churches, the school, the garage, the inn or even friends and neighbours. Some did use cars, motor bikes or pedal cycles for those short trips, but many of them walked.

The hill was on a busy B-class road that carried traffic into Ashfordly from places as far as York but also from far-off towns such as Leeds and others in various parts of the West Riding. Aidensfield Bank became extremely busy during the summer tourist season or when some of the other roads, including Sutton Bank, were closed.

Sutton Bank was often shut either for repairs or due to snow but it was also notorious because caravan drivers became stuck or lorries were unable to cope with the gradients if they got behind slow drivers and caravans. Happily and sensibly, caravans have since been banned from Sutton Bank—they caused untold numbers of blockages. Aidensfield Bank itself had a gradient of 1-in-5 with a very steep and sharp turn at the foot, aggravated by an exit onto an equally busy road at the summit. In fact, my Beat Report showed that the bottom of Aidensfield Bank, where the village street entered it, was an accident black spot, and so was the summit where the bank's carriageway opened onto a busy through-road.

Very soon after my arrival at Aidensfield and while I still had boundless enthusiasm, I had submitted a report which high-lighted these problems and dangers and suggested a footpath be constructed down the full length of the hill with a view to increasing road safety. I recommended that it should be wide enough to accommodate young mothers with children and prams, children with bikes and other people who might be walking that way alone or with company, especially dogs. I thought elderly folk and children were particularly vulnerable. I asked that my report be forwarded to the Clerk of the County Council so that the necessary department could be informed—I hoped that one of their experts would visit the scene, consider the evidence, take a census of traffic both vehicular and pedestrian, obtain accident statistics from the Accident Prevention Department over the past ten years and then hopefully construct the path.

I submitted my report through what are called *the usual channels*. This meant it went to Ashfordly Police Station for the sergeant to read, absorb and add any pertinent comments. From there he would send it to the inspector at Eltering who would consider the contents and add his own comments before forwarding it to the Superintendent at Malton. If the Superintendent approved of my suggestion, it would be despatched to Police Headquarters for the chief constable to initial it—that indicated he knew what was going on in the county—and it was just possible he might order the Accident Prevention Department to add its own comments and relevant statistics before sending it to the Clerk of the County Council. He was in charge of all the departments at County Hall and would refer the report to the necessary office, the one that dealt with pavements positioned beside roads and not merely footpaths that ran through rural landscapes. That would surely be the Highways Department at local level and not a Government department.

And having done that piece of valuable work, I settled down to wait. I never heard another thing about my proposal, not even from the sergeant nor others in the chain of police command, and certainly nothing emanated from County Hall. Such a silence was not unusual and I knew it was not within my remit to remind everyone of my suggestion—these things took time. There was nothing I could do but wait. With the passage of time and with other duty matters to concern me, however, I forgot about that suggestion and it was when clearing out my desk as I prepared to move house that I found the carbon copy of that old report. And I was shocked to be reminded that nothing had been done. I should have done something about it by now—perhaps I should have risked antagonising my superiors by issuing a second proposal just in case the first had got lost in the vast corridors of local authority power? I stared at the piece of paper and wondered whether anyone had read it.

The fact was that no footpath had appeared on Aidensfield Bank and so I decided I would shake County Hall and the local police administrative system to their foundations by re-submitting the report. I would provide many more facts and figures along with some more detailed research.

This might be the means by which the villagers would remember me—my very own contribution to the safety and security of Aidensfield!

In my second report, which was written some four years after the first, I referred to that first one and knew that that action alone would cause much consternation among filing clerks in County Hall and Police Headquarters as they searched for my first missive. I knew how the admin systems functioned because when anyone referred to an earlier file or document, it had to be found and attached to the most recent one. By forcing that very simple device to be completed, someone had to take notice of my second attempt. If my original report could not be found, then I would be asked for a copy of it because everyone along its official route into some filing system or other would want to know what it had contained. In that way, therefore, I would make sure someone actually considered my suggestion and so I got to work. It might be the last report I completed before leaving Aidensfield.

This time I conducted a vehicle count on the hill, selecting at random a half-hour period in mid-morning one Wednesday. In uniform I established myself prominently at the side of the road near the bottom of the hill and counted every vehicle travelling up and down. I used a special form I had devised. One effect of my presence was to cause the drivers to slow down even though I was not conducting a speed check. It probably looked as if that was my task because I was using an official-looking clipboard to hold my piece of paper. I hoped Claude Jeremiah Greengrass would pass by with his "dog cart" even if I did not have a box to cater for that means of transport.

I had spaces to tick for service buses, touring buses, articulated lorries, pantechnicons, ordinary lorries, dust carts, fire appliances, mobile cranes, military tanks, cattle trucks and horseboxes, vans, cars towing caravans, cars not towing caravans, taxis, tractors with trailers, tractors without trailers, track-laying vehicles, agricultural machines such as binders and combine harvesters, horse-drawn vehicles, motor bikes, pedal cycles and other hand-drawn vehicles like prams or handcarts. I also included a column for 'Other vehicles' that might have included motor mowers, invalid carriages or dumper trucks. And, of course, I included pedestrians.

And within that half-hour, I noted forty-nine assorted vehicles on the bank and that resulted in 98 per hour during a time that was not particularly busy—well over one each minute on average. Thus in, say, a twelve-hour period, we might expect 1176 vehicles but I felt that the same calculation would not work for a 24-hour-spell—there'd be fewer vehicles at night. I did wonder, however, just how many vehicles, and of what variety, passed up and down that bank at peak holiday times, or when Sutton Bank was closed. Certainly it was busier than I expected during my test period.

As I was conducting my survey, Mrs Potiphar walked past and gave me a brief smile.

'I'm looking for Greengrass,' I told her.

'Thank goodness you are doing something about that man, constable,' and off she went.

My next task was to list all the vulnerable people who might have to walk that distance from the village to the bank top, or vice versa. One house at the side of the road on the hill was occupied by a 70-year-old man without a car; another householder was an 85-year-old woman who needed a walking stick to support her. Three couples were in the age-bracket 55-60 and in houses at the bank top there were nine children under the age of 10, not to mention the grandchildren of some residents who walked up the hill at weekends to visit them. For all those local people, walking up and down the hill involved heavy risks because there was nowhere to walk in safety and no means of escaping from the highway in an emergency. Steep upward-sloping grass banks at either side of the road made that impossible. Anyone walking on that section of road was therefore at risk, but some of the local people had no alternative.

And so I produced a report full of facts, figures and assumptions and, even though there was no record of a fatal traffic accident on the hill, I suggested such an event was becoming increasingly likely due to the growing number of vehicles and pedestrians likely to walk that hazardous route. In addition to local inhabitants, the road was also used by hikers and cyclists. I even obtained supporting letters from some of the families who used the stretch of road and produced details of all recorded traffic accidents on it over the last ten years. Although none was fatal, forty-two had been recorded and of these six had been described as serious.

Feeling very proud of myself, I planned to submit my report as my last act before leaving Aidensfield. Then one day in the future I would return to see whether anyone had taken any notice of it. If not, then I would ensure the officials would receive another reminder. Or maybe I could persuade our local Member of Parliament to take up the cause? I did not think that I, as a police officer, could lobby an MP on such a matter, but I knew someone who would.

And so I forwarded my report through official channels and settled down to await the outcome as I continued my search for a house and for the elusive Claude Jeremiah Greengrass.

CHAPTER 4

Before leaving my police house at Aidensfield on any routine patrol, I had to either telephone or radio Ashfordly Police Station so that I was shown as being 'on duty.' In this way, the office constable knew who was patrolling, along with the area in which he was operating. By that means, he could direct any of us to an incident such as a traffic accident, sudden death, housebreaking and so forth, and he could also acquaint us with any messages about such things as stolen vehicles, missing persons and suspects on the run whether on my beat or away from it.

One morning, I telephoned at 10am to say that, after an hour's office duty, I was about to embark upon a routine patrol of my beat. Alf Ventress, as usual, answered my call.

'Understood, Nick. Only one message—we've had a report of a black cat in Whinstone Woods. I mean a big cat, not a pussy, something like a puma. It was glimpsed early this morning by a hiker who's alerted us. You'd expect him to be fairly reliable. The press is being informed to warn the public to keep their distance, but we've no reports of escapes from any of the local zoos or country estates.'

'Thanks, Alf. This isn't the first of these big cats to be seen around here, is it?'

'No, we've had lots of reports over the past months but no positive sightings, footmarks nor droppings. Whether it's folks seeing things or whether they're genuine, we can't be sure. We just need to be cautious.'

'Thanks, Alf, I won't attempt to stroke it! I'm off to Ploatby now.'

But were pumas coloured black? I thought they were tawny or perhaps grey.

Anyway, I parked the van so I could complete a foot patrol around the hamlet of Ploatby and perhaps locate Greengrass but instead found myself dealing with a lady who had a curious problem. Ploatby was one of the smaller villages on my patch.

I had visited two farms to check their stock registers before deciding to stroll along to the western end of the village and then back again. Such apparently aimless patrolling was in fact a well-tested means of presenting the uniform which was both a reassuring sight for the general public but also a good means of crime prevention even if it did not achieve anything dramatic. It was a highly visible means of showing that the police were available and that in itself was reassuring to many people. I must be honest, however, and say that another reason for my patrolling was that I wanted to see whether any cottages or houses were for sale or even to rent in this peaceful place.

The road through Ploatby was a simple diversion from the main road and I wondered if this was the kind of road Claude would use for driving his "dog cart"? It had once been a main road but many years ago, a by-pass had been thought necessary due to a narrow and very ancient hump-back bridge near the east end of the village. Rather than demolish or widen the historic bridge, a by-pass had been sanctioned and it now meant the village did not have to tolerate the masses of tourists who flocked in their buses, cars and caravans to the nearby honey pots. They all drove past the road-end with few, if any, considering the turn to this small place. It meant that Ploatby had not lost its enviable tranquillity and charm which was perhaps one reason why it was full of incomers and very few locally born people. With no shop, post office, inn or church it was indeed very quiet.

As I walked along the street, which was little more than half a mile long, I was not particularly seeking crime and criminals as I concentrated upon finding 'For Sale' signs on houses. I did not really expect to find one because none of the local estates had featured any in their current sales brochures and in any case, houses rarely came on the market in Ploatby. If one was for sale, news was invariably passed by word-of-mouth but most curiously and very unexpectedly I did find one.

It was on the northern side of the village and roughly halfway between the Thackerston road junction and Ploatby Manor. Substantially built in local yellow limestone, the house looked well-kept and spacious with a red pantiled roof while the 'For Sale' sign was standing in a well-tended front garden. A name sign announced the house was Battle Hall and a wide tarmac drive led from the street and passed along the side of the house into the extensive grounds behind. I could see a double garage at the rear with evidence of a larger patch of land beyond a gate—some trees were showing above the house from where I stood and so I reckoned there were fields and even a copse at the rear. The 'For Sale' sign did not give any indication of the size or the extent of its accommodation neither did it display any estate agent's name or the asking price. By examining the property from the street, I guessed it was a spacious five or six bed-roomed detached house with a double garage and several acres of land. There was no doubt it would be far beyond my modest means, but I was interested nonetheless—I considered it wise to examine lots of other houses of all types before selecting one for the family.

I had been aware of this house since my arrival as the village bobby at Aidensfield but had never had any reason to call. It had formerly been a farmhouse with several hundred acres of land. It was a private house and most of its land had been sold, except for a few acres. I had often wondered why it was called Battle Hall for I had found no evidence or records of a battle or even a minor skirmish on this site. However, local folklore and persistent rumours said a famous battle had once occurred there, but a distinct lack of evidence or historical data in any of my files or reference books suggested this was more than a rumour.

The longer I examined Battle Hall from a distance, the more I appreciated how far beyond my reach it would be. Although, I recognized the wisdom of buying the most expensive and largest house one could afford, there were limits! A policeman's salary did not lend itself to buying and maintaining such a large and impressive property, but, I told myself, there was no harm in looking!

So should I knock on the door to find out precisely what price was being asked? Maybe I would be invited inside to have a look around and assess the accommodation? Or maybe the house could be available for rent in the short term?

The occupier was clearly at home—I could see a car in the garage whose doors were standing open. I must admit I stood and stared for a quite a long time, no doubt causing local residents to wonder why the constabulary was paying such close attention to that house. It was while I dithered that the front door opened and small woman appeared. I guessed she would be in her late sixties or early seventies.

'Hello,' she called across the front garden. 'Hello, is that the policeman? Are you looking for something? Or is it the postman? I haven't got my right specs on.'

'Yes, it's the policeman, PC Rhea from Aidensfield,' I confirmed in a loud voice as I took a few strides closer.

'And I am Lucy Broughton, Mrs Lucy Broughton. I'm so glad I saw you standing there, I was about to ring you. How odd that you should be right outside my house at this very moment. Just by chance I saw you when I went to make my call.'

'Yes, very odd,' I agreed, wondering if fortune was about to shine upon me.

I let myself in through the small latch gate and approached the house, removing my cap as I did so. As I drew nearer, I noticed the windows did not have curtains and the entire ground floor appeared to be empty—no carpets, no furniture; nothing in fact. I felt I had to apologize for my rudeness in staring at the house.

'I hope you don't mind, but I was admiring your house as I was passing. I see it's for sale.'

She was a slender woman about five feet two inches tall with grey hair and a very clean skin. In her younger days, she would have been a great beauty, I was sure.

Now she was dressed in a pair of old grey slacks and a paint-smattered smock, looking very much the country woman at work.

'I don't mind at all, Mr Rhea, after all it is for sale. Are you interested?'

'I'm looking for a good family house, I've got four children but I think this would be beyond my means.'

'There's no harm in looking but I have to tell you it is almost certain the house has been spoken for,' she smiled sweetly. 'But by all means have a look around just in case things don't work out as planned. Follow me and I will tell you why I was on the point of calling you. We'll start with the kitchen where I shall be delighted to offer you a mug of tea and a scone. It's so nice to have a visitor.'

'It's a deal!'

I followed her inside and our footsteps echoed in the empty house as we moved through the spacious hall into the big lounge.

'Empty, you see, all empty, it echoes a lot now,' she waved her hands to indicate the void around us. It reminded me of a similar house I had once encountered in Briggsby where the owner had lost her cat shortly before moving out. Here I could see where pictures had hung from the walls and where furniture had rested in front of the wallpaper. It had produced dark patterns where sunlight had faded parts of it. She led me to the distant end of the lounge and through double doors into the kitchen with its Aga and some fittings still in position. But the Aga was cold and so she filled an electric kettle and switched it on.

I felt the whole place exuded an air of desertion.

'I'm sure I don't need to take you around the entire house, Mr Rhea, because it is all like this, all empty and deserted, most of my belongings have gone to my new house but you are welcome to have a look around on your own if you wish. There are six good bedrooms upstairs, a bathroom and two separate toilets. Two of the bedrooms have washbasins: very handy for guests. I'm moving out tomorrow, you see, to my new home in the Cotswolds. A small van will be coming in the morning to take away my final oddments, all that is left here—my bed and some clothing and other bits and pieces.'

'It's always sad, having to move,' I tried to think of something sensible to say while not being inquisitive or intrusive.

'It is, and more-so because I am just cleaning up and tidying what is left, putting touches of paint here and there, making it smart for the new owner—if he ever gets here.'

She had not yet told me why she was about to ring the police but I was prepared to wait; clearly she wanted to explain about her impending departure.

'It's a big house, Mrs Broughton,' I stated the obvious. 'Ideal for a family.'

'Apart from the six good bedrooms, Mr Rhea, there is a large lounge, this kitchen, a pantry, the entrance hall, a drawing room, a dining room, utility room, good attic and large cellar. Double garage and four acres of land, there are fields behind the house. There used to be more when this was a farm—well over a hundred and fifty acres, but that was sold before we moved in. We couldn't have coped with all that land, but now the house itself has become too big for me since my husband died. None of my children wants it, it is too isolated for any of them, they need to be near the town for work. The sale is not being handled by local estate agents because my late husband's company is overseeing it. And it's all for only £7,500. I might add that my 'For Sale' sign in the front garden has produced a great deal of interest and I must tell you that there is one man who is extremely anxious to buy the property. He has made a good offer but he must sell his own first in order to secure this one. That has not yet happened, there is some kind of delay. I have no clear idea of his ability to proceed but I am determined to move out so there will be vacant possession which is always a good selling point. My new home is waiting and happily I do not need a mortgage—the sale of this one can wait a month or two. I am not desperate by any means, but common sense says that if a good offer comes along from someone else, I should take it.'

'I hope it all works out for you and I'm not surprised there's been a lot of interest, it's a lovely place.'

'I have had a constant stream of visitors, most of them being nothing more than snoopers, pretending to be interested while all they wanted was a look around the house and perhaps a free cup of tea and a biscuit. I'm not including you in that category, by the way, I called you!'

'I have to be honest with you,' I said with a degree of sadness. 'Quite simply I can't afford this kind of price, neither could I afford the upkeep! There is no need for me to look around and I am so pleased you've found a buyer, even if he is taking his time.'

'Well I want to talk to you anyway, so let's sit down and enjoy a cup of tea and some cake.'

As I settled at the table she placed a plate of fruitcake before me and a couple of mugs. The kettle was singing and she stood beside it, waiting for the water to boil as she said. 'So you must be wondering why I want to talk to you?'

'Yes but I'm in no great hurry to find out.'

'Does the name of this house mean anything to you, Mr Rhea?'

'Battle Hall? It sounds as if this plot was an ancient battlefield. I did some research after I arrived at Aidensfield, but didn't come across any past battles on this site or anywhere else in Ploatby. I've no idea how the name arose.'

She made the tea and brought the pot over to the table to settled down opposite. 'That's what we thought, Mr Rhea, my late husband and I. It's a logical assumption. When we bought the house, the name intrigued us so we undertook the usual local research, but found no record of a battlefield on this site. We didn't give up, though, and began to ask the local residents—and then we discovered that during the seventeenth, eighteenth and early nineteenth centuries, the house used to be called Battle Royal Hall but no one I spoke to knew why. Most of the people in this village are incomers with little or no knowledge of local history. But quite obviously there had to be a reason for such a name and for the change of name.'

'You considered a royal connection?'

'I must admit that is what we thought. Our researches indicated that over the centuries a number of battles had been fought not far from here—Towton, Myton, Stamford Bridge, Fulford, Marston Moor, Ebberston, Byland and probably others that are lost to history. And in the distant past, kings did travel widely and often stayed in large village houses during their tours or when indulging in battles. Anyway, some time before we bought it, the 'Royal' part of the name was dropped and it became simply Battle Hall.'

As she was explaining, something occurred to me. I recalled some of the ancient laws that had outlawed the cruel, but highly popular sport of cockfighting.

I had written pieces about the laws that had led to its prohibition, and one of the terms used was 'battle royal.' Fighting birds from one area would form a team to compete with those from other areas, and those birds were known as a main. Each bird took its turn to fight a member of an opposing team and they fought in this way until only one was left. He represented the winning team and that battle was called a battle royal, inevitably accompanied by heavy betting. Several attempts had been made to ban the practice, although evidence of the sport remains in some places. There is evidence both in isolated sites on the moors surrounding Aidensfield and in some low-land villages.

On a wider scale, until 1816 there had been a Royal Cockpit on Birdcage Walk in London, one near the Houses of Parliament and another called New Cockpit Royal in Little Grosvenor Street in Westminster, London. Perhaps the most prestigious was the one in St James' Park, London. Cockfighting was long regarded as very fashionable with many cockpits around the whole of rural Britain, some later being concealed in barns after the sport had been outlawed. In some areas, reminders are still visible to the knowledgeable eye but it was the closure of the St James' Park cockpit in 1816 that was perhaps responsible for rendering the sport unfashionable.

In 1835, the Cruelty to Animals Act prohibited cock-fighting in England and in 1837, the ban was extended to Ireland, nonetheless adherents continued to practise the sport in secret with many cockpits being concealed in iso-lated barns. Tougher laws were passed in 1849 but by 1862, there was evidence that cockfighting was continuing despite the law. Prosecutions did follow yet the sport thrived in secret and another attempt to ban it was contained in the Protection of Animals Act 1911. That was reinforced yet again by the Cockfight Act of 1952 but it is claimed that it has continued in secret places.

Much of this flashed through my mind as we chatted, and I gave my host some of those facts moments before real-izing the significance of the Hall's former name. Battle Royal Hall.

'It's to do with cockfighting, isn't it?' I ventured. 'Battle Royal.'

'Absolutely,' she smiled. 'And I think they dropped Royal from the name when it became both unfashionable and illegal. But the old cockpit is still here, in one of the fields behind our house. It still belongs to this property.'

'Really? Is that where they keep finding old coins? And things like steel gaffles and leather hoods?' I had come across talk of such things in local pubs—odds and ends kept turn-ing up during ploughing or building work but they were of no interest to the police because, not being made of gold or silver, they did not constitute a treasure trove.

'Some of those things were found around our fields, Mr Rhea, because it was a major centre for cockfights, especially battles royal. And that brings me neatly to the reason I was going to ring you.'

'This sounds intriguing!'

'It took us a long time to ferret out all the information associated with cockfighting. Most of it happened long before the birth of even our oldest residents but folk memories had been retained in some of them, although as I said earlier, most of the people here do not have their origins in the area. Verbal history was—and is—in short supply, Mr Rhea. Not surprisingly, there's nothing about it in local history books either because it was such a secretive sport; it was almost like a secret wartime movement, and modern historians know so little about it. However, we discovered that a classic battle royal took place here about 1805 and so Hall Farm, as it was then called, became a place of pilgrimage for adherents.

'That particular battle became something of a legend among the cockfighting fraternity both locally and further afield and so the farm's name was changed. From being Hall Farm it became Battle Royal Hall.'

'That explains a lot,' I agreed.

'It was certainly a famous venue and cockfights contin-ued here long after the sport was banned. I have to say though, that although I've lived here for more than thirty years, I can honestly say we've never hosted one on our premises nor does anyone living in the village know of any such events, even though they might be continuing in secret in some places. Or perhaps they are not admitting their knowledge!'

'It's quite a history, Mrs Broughton, I do hope you've written most of it down for the future,' I was enjoying this conversation and her company. 'We've learned something today.'

'Indeed we have, and I have written up some notes for our local museum. And now the reason why I was going to ring you was because of the links between this house and cockfighting.'

'But I thought it had all ended a long time ago?'

'The fighting did but not the association with the sport.'

'Really? This is getting more intriguing,' I had now reached the end of my mug of tea and she was quick to drain hers.

She rose from the table saying, 'Follow me, Mr Rhea, we're going into the fields behind the house. As I said, they are being sold along with the property, but the one we are going to visit is quite different and very interesting.'

She led me through the back kitchen door then out into the garden. Everything was neat and well-tended, a nice vegetable garden. Everything for the new owner lay to one side as we continued across the garden via a gravel path and through a hand-gate into the field. After about a hundred yards she stopped and pointed. 'There you are. After what we have just been saying, you'll know what that is?'

She was indicating a large basin-like depression in the ground that at first glance looked like an empty pond that had been grassed over. It was a complete circle and would be about ten yards in diameter and it seemed the earth excavated from the basin had been arranged around the outer rim to form a barrier. In the centre was a small mound of earth covered with grass and I thought it looked well maintained.

'It's a cockpit,' I announced, feeling proud of my knowledge. 'The audience would sit around the edge on that high rim, sometimes in tiers or even on seats while the birds fought their battles in the bottom or upon that mound. Some contestants waited in barns and large buildings, out of sight, and in many cases there were such barns near the cockpits. Fights would also take place in barns, if secrecy was vital, or if the weather was very bad.'

'Right,' she smiled. 'When we bought this house, it was a condition that we didn't fill in that pit. We had no idea what it was or why that clause was in the purchase agreement. At first we thought it was a pond but it is so well-drained that water never gathers there. So quite unknowingly we bought a cockpit. I would imagine it is quite rare—not many houses will have a cockpit.'

'That's true, but you've never used it? For anything at all?'

'No, never, not even as a piece of ornamental garden or a pond. And certainly not for cockfighting. I'm against the sport and once I found out the truth I questioned the validity of that clause but was told it was a condition of purchase to which we had agreed. It meant we had to leave the pit as it was, as you see it now. And that is why I wanted to talk to you.'

She began to stroll around the circumference of the pit, pointing out several distant farm-gates that provided entrances to and exits from the field. 'Those gates led from and into the adjoining land,' she explained. 'When the spectators arrived, they came in by a range of different routes and afterwards left via those gates, so they were unrecognized as a crowd while here, and they dispersed over a wide area as they left. You could get a hundred men here and no one could see them, there was no entrance or exit through our garden at that time. So they avoided discovery.'

'So you're saying that *illegal* cockfighting was practised here?'

'It must have been, if they took such precautions to safeguard their activities.'

'Hmm, it's all very interesting, Mrs Broughton, quite fascinating so does it mean that when you sell the house, the cockpit goes with it? With those same conditions?'

'It does, Mr Rhea, which is why I wanted this chat,' and she began to walk around the edge of the field, which was down to grass, quite dry and clean.

She remained silent for a while then said, 'I hope I am not being silly or making a nuisance of myself, but regularly over the years while we've been here, men have assembled around that cockpit. Certainly they never sought permission to assemble on our land. They came along those old routes into the cockpit field, using ancient footpaths and rights of way. So far as we could tell, they were not breaking any laws, neither were they trespassing.'

'So have you any idea why they came?'

'As I said earlier, my husband and I thought it was some kind of pilgrimage by adherents to cockfighting, coming to see where the famous battle royal had occurred but still keeping their activities very secret.'

'They've never actually revived it here, have they?' was my obvious question.

'I don't think so, I think we'd have heard them shouting and noticed a lot of noise, but they were always quiet and well-behaved, they even took their litter away.'

'But surely they were trespassing? They didn't have your permission?'

'No, they used old paths and routes all with rights of way, so they weren't trespassing and didn't require our consent to assemble. As I said, they never asked for permission but neither did they explain their presence. They just turned up out of the blue. On one occasion my husband's curiosity get the better of him so he went over and asked them what was going on. One of them said his great-grandfather had always come here to attend the cockfights and had been present during that famous battle royal. He said most of the other men could claim a similar link. The man said they came here once a year on the first Saturday in September and all they did was sit around the pit and talk over sandwiches and a few bottles of beer. It seems their forefathers had done so for years past but we did not object—they were no trouble.'

'So once you've gone, we can expect a band of men to turn up one Saturday in September and do likewise? Sit around the cockpit and reminisce about their ancestors and cockfighting?'

'Yes, Mr Rhea, but I do stress they tend the site and keep it clean but I thought the police should know about this odd happening just in case a crowd of men turn up after I've gone and while the house is still empty.'

'Well, I can't see they are breaking the law and provided the new owner doesn't object, there's little we can do. The laws on civil trespass do not involve the police.'

'I won't object because I will not be here,' she stressed.

'So a lot depends upon the attitude of any new owner? And that curious clause continues to feature in the sale agreement?'

'It does indeed, Mr Rhea.'

As we patrolled the edge of the field, making a circular tour around the cockpit, I could see she was preoccupied.

'There's something else, isn't there?' I put to her.

'You're very perceptive.'

'Does the regular arrival of those men trouble you?' I asked.

'It didn't, not until I met the man who is negotiating to buy this house. I recognized him from an old press cutting. He'd been fined in Wakefield a few years ago, for organizing cockfights. His name is Whittaker, John Whittaker. When he came to look around the house, the first thing he wanted to see was the old cockpit which he knew about, and he came up with the tale that his ancestors had attended it, when the sport was legal. He said he had often come here on that annual pilgrimage and, of course, he intends to be the new owner of this house—and that cockpit.'

'You think he might be planning to revive the sport here in Ploatby? Is that what you are saying?'

'I think the police should be aware of the possibility,' she was very diplomatic. 'There are many factors that make it all so feasible, Mr Rhea. I can't say it will happen, of course, no one can. But I think that you, as the local constable along with your colleagues should be alerted to the possibility.'

'I agree,' I told her. 'That is exactly the kind of advance information that we need. Thank you for being so astute.'

'Does my name have to appear in your records?'

'No, we can treat it as intelligence received without revealing the source and, with Whittaker's name, we can check his record before he arrives. But we will keep watch, I assure you, even though I shall not be part of the team.'

I explained about my imminent departure but assured her that the Ashfordly team of constables would honour my agreement and keep a watchful eye on Battle Hall. I would make sure they were fully informed and that the necessary records were up to date. However, in the years that followed, I never heard of any raids on the old cockpit nor any rumours of a revival of cockfighting at Battle Hall. Perhaps Mr Whittaker merely wanted the old house so that it could be a permanent shrine in honour of times past? I shall never know.

* * *

There is no doubt that the names of houses provide endless entertainment and speculation. How and why they come to be blessed with curious names is of constant interest.

The most fascinating are those that digress from oft-used and very common names such as Dunroamin, River View Cottage or Karrinamore, the latter being the home of a bricklayer's retired labourer. Some are the result of much deep thought and guile and a glance through a telephone directory will reveal hundreds of intriguing titles for streets as well as houses.

While patrolling my expansive rural beat I came across many interesting examples and it is perhaps wise to remind ourselves that, out in the country and certainly on the moors around Aidensfield, there are very few streets.

Many rural houses are therefore not numbered, but carry names instead. Lots are farms or large country houses and so we find many bearing the name of Manor, Hall, Park, Grange, House, Lodge, Bank, Hill or Head as in Dale Head. My beat had dozens of farms bearing such names. A number of the villages had large houses prefixed by the village name with the suffix of Manor, Lodge, House or Hall. For example, there was Aidensfield Lodge, Elsinby Lodge and Briggsby Lodge. Each of those impressive houses had a farm nearby called Lodge Farm. Thus there was Lodge Farm, Aidensfield; Lodge Farm, Elsinby and Lodge Farm, Briggsby. In addition there were Bank Farms at Graindale, Seavham and Stovensby, and Hill Farms at Briggsby, Craydale and Slemmington. There is no doubt that the frequent use of identical names in different villages caused confusion among visitors and some deliverymen. Sometimes, the wrong Hill Farm would be visited and this could be aggravated when one farm was called East Hill Farm and another nearby was West Hill Farm, both with the same village address. Hall Farm and Hill Farm were often confused too. Another example was that the postal address of Maddleskirk Abbey was simply Maddleskirk Abbey, York. Not surprisingly, it was common for delivery vehicles to arrive in York to ask for directions, only to be told that the abbey was twenty miles away.

However, as the village constable of Aidensfield it was my duty to know the whereabouts of all farms and houses and on many occasions it was an interesting exercise to delve into the reason for their names. Most were inherited from past centuries such as Priory Farm, Abbey House, Castle Lodge, Witch Hill, Quarry Side Farm, Highdale, Spring Farm, Hilltop and Hall Farm. They would be called by those names long before the written word became commonplace.

Many were intriguing such as Cat-Hanging Farm, Starvemouse Farm, Gosling Mire, Tuft House, Peep o' Day, Rise o' Day, Morn o' Day, Flower o' Day, Bumper Castle, Bog Hall, Throstle Nest and Cuckoo's Nest. The latter must give rise to speculation as to its origins because cuckoos do not have nests—they lay their eggs in the nests of other birds. Many of the names were relatively simple—there were lots of Home Farms, for example, their names deriving from their parent manor or stately home, along with frequently used names like Wood End Farm, Village Farm, Rock Head Farm, High Moor Farm, Low Moor Farm, Crag Farm, Mill Farm, Dale Farm, Prospect Farm, Riverside Farm and so forth.

At Maddleskirk, however, the village adjoining Aidensfield, there was always confusion between Main Street and High Street.

The main street that ran through the centre of the village contained the shop, post office, garage, two inns, two chapels, two churches, a school, three farms, lots of cottages and several large houses. The High Street, however, was about a mile from the village where it crossed the higher moors. It had a couple of farms along its route. The name High Street resulted from that isolated track's former history as a Roman road but the name did—and still does—cause confusion. Delivery men still spend ages seeking High Street while driving along Main Street—and it is not there and never has been during the past 2,000 years or so. Incidentally, the suffix 'le street' in a village name indicates that it formerly stood upon a Roman road.

The puzzles provided by such discrepancies made it sensible for me to familiarise myself with all these addresses and so I did with the help of a large-scale map on the wall of the office in my police house. Having found the required name, I made a point of visiting the establishment in the hope I would never forget its location, but even so there were times I had to check my map just to be certain.

But I was stumped one Tuesday morning. The phone rang and a man's voice asked, 'Is that the Constable?'

'Yes, PC Rhea speaking,' I assured him.

'I wondered if you could spare the time to come and look at something I've found, and give me some advice.'

I could not place his accent which was definitely not from any part of Yorkshire or the north-east; it was what might be described as standard English speech, the sort you might encounter in a radio talk or interview, and quite devoid of any regional accent. From that, I assumed he was not a local person.

'Yes of course. So what do you want me to look at?'

'Well, Constable, I am not sure what the object is but it might be gold which is why I'm calling you. I suspect it might be treasure trove and want to do the right thing.'

'Well, I can't decide whether a thing is gold or not, that will require an expert's examination but I can come along to advise you on the procedures associated with such finds.'

'Good, then when can I expect you?'

'I have to call at my section office in Ashfordly with some files and then I am free to join you. So where do I find you?'

'Salutation in High Rannockdale, Constable. The name is Carson, Joseph Carson.'

I had never come across that address during all my time as the constable of Aidensfield and paused briefly as I searched my wall map for it. In addition to farms and mansions, some small premises might be shown on the map, particularly if they were very isolated. But I could not find Salutation House or Salutation Farm.

'Hello, are you still there?'

'Sorry, Mr Carson, I was trying to find your house on my map. I've never come across that name before.'

'But you know Rannockdale?'

'I do indeed, but I've never been to Salutation House, Farm or Inn.'

'Not Salutation House, Farm or Inn, Mr Rhea. Just Salutation. You turn off the road as you enter Rannockdale from the south. Turn first left down a short track, the building is out of sight behind a small copse, not a metalled road . . . it's got a slate roof. It's the only one along that track so you can't miss it. The track continues over the hills behind High Rannockdale where it is unsurfaced and full of pot-holes. It crosses the moors until it drops into Rockdale. It's very remote up here but very quiet which is why I bought the building. That was fairly recently, I'm from the south so this is all new country to me. But the building is very ancient with few written records and I'm renovating it, with all the necessary consents, I might add.'

'So it is a house?'

'More like a barn but I'm turning it into a house and studio.'

'Oh, I see. So what have you found?'

'I'm not sure. It's very dirty but it looks like gold which is why I called you.'

'Well, I should be with you in three-quarters of an hour or so.'

73

'I'll get the kettle on and my car is parked outside, a dark blue Jaguar, it's highly visible,'

'Thank you, see you then,' and so I rang off.

The journey into Rannockdale was always a pleasure due to its remote location coupled with the splendid views from the access road.

High Rannockdale was locally known as a most remote and deserted place, so much so that I had never had cause to visit it. Nothing ever happened there apart from the activities of wild life, but now I had a reason to pay my very first official visit.

As I drove the mini-van across the moors, I marvelled at the scenery and felt privileged to have been able to work in such splendid and interesting surroundings. I wondered whether the reported big cat would wander as far as this from Whinstone Wood but I doubted it—much of the landscape around here was wide open moorland whereas I felt sure the animal would favour shelter in the woods.

As I approached Rannockdale, I turned left as indicated by Mr Carson and within fifteen minutes or so found myself approaching his premises. It was a large structure in dark grey granite with a blue slate roof and I noticed it had no windows. My first impression was that it looked very forbidding and far from attractive, and I was comforted to see the blue Jaguar parked outside. I eased my little police van into a space beside the big car, booked off the air and approached the house. There was a large barn-like entrance with double doors, one of which was standing open to admit some light. As I approached, a tall man appeared from inside and smiled a welcome. With fair hair and blue eyes, he was dressed in white overalls that were smothered in paint of various colours but he did not carry a paint brush. Somehow he looked smart despite his dress. I guessed he would be in his late forties.

'Ah, you must be PC Rhea. Welcome, I'm Carson. My friends call me Joe and I regard you as a friend, being the local bobby.'

'That's kind of you.' My first impressions were that this was a genuinely nice man. 'I'm Nick.'

'Then once I have finished this project, you must join me for a meal. But first, come inside and have a look.'

He led me into the dark interior and the place reminded me of the banqueting hall of a medieval castle in both size and shape. It was one huge cavern with no upper rooms but with a massive and spectacular beamed roof and then, as my eyes became accustomed to the windowless gloom, I realized the place had once been divided into smaller units. The floor comprised packed and dry earth and was littered with old wooden beams, stones, bales of straw and what looked like discarded farm machinery.

'I don't live here yet,' he told me as he led me towards the distant end. 'While I'm working here, I've cobbled up a bed-space with a camp bed, and my kitchen is little more than a Primus stove with a kettle and umpteen tins of beans. There's no running water—I rely on the beck for that—and no electricity. It's more primitive than camping when I was a Boy Scout, but I get by. As they say, it will be nice when it's finished.'

In the space he used as a kitchen there was a 1940s cabinet, a battered table, two old chairs and when I arrived, he lit the Primus stove and almost immediately, the kettle began to sing.

'I warmed it up before you came,' he smiled. 'Coffee all right? Sit down and we can chat.' After producing the coffee—black—he settled down at the table and began. 'First, I'd better explain all this,' and he waved his arms to emphasize the sheer space. 'I'm a composer and I want to build a state-of-the-art studio with modern recording equipment so that is my project. A studio and dwelling house combined. Obviously there's a massive amount of work to do from the floor upwards, I need to install large windows, an upper floor, damp proofing, sound proofing, new inner walls, water, heating, electricity, sewage, drains, the lot in fact, even new foundations in places . . . but I've had this old place tested and it is surprisingly sound and dry. Clearly, I shall not do everything myself, I will commission contractors when I am ready, but there's a lot I can do in the meantime. There will be no problems with the planners who welcome sympathetic conversions that bring old buildings back into use rather than allow them to become ruinous. The only condition to date is that I sound-proof my building so that the noise of music or bands is not a nuisance outside. I'll build a small flat into the structure so I can live here. So there we are. I'm trying to produce a good draft design before I commit myself to architects and builders.'

'So what did this used to be?' I asked.

'No one seems to know, Nick. There are no records but the nearest I got to finding out something was that, way back in medieval times, there was a priory in High Rannockdale.'

'I had no idea, I thought I knew the location of all our monasteries, ruined or otherwise.'

'This one did not even survive long enough for Henry VIII to knock it down. Not a stone remains—they've all been used to build farms and houses on these moors. So far as I can see, when the priory failed, a local landowner bought the premises and the land, then sold the stone to local builders.'

'But this place wasn't knocked down?'

'No, it was sold, several times, so I believe. I think it belonged to the old monastery but there are no records so it is all guesswork. I bought it from a local farmer whose ancestors had owned it for years and years, without really using it except as a place of storage for unwanted machinery and rubbish.'

'It could have been a tithe barn,' I suggested. 'They needed to be spacious and dry, and it was the sort of thing a monastery or parish church would use to store their donated piles of grain, hay, crops and so on.'

'So why call it Salutation if it was nothing more than a barn?' he asked. 'That's what baffles me. Anyway, here we are—now let me show you my trophy.'

He went over to the kitchen cabinet, opened a drawer and drew out a dirty gold-coloured article of some kind. He laid it before me and I saw it comprised an oval shape fashioned from metal and about six inches wide by eight inches long. It was adorned with grooves that made it appear to be made from spikes. They could have even depicted rays of sunshine or other lights and they protruded for a short distance over the edge of the entire design to give it a slightly irregular appearance.

Its general shape was oval if a little jagged. In the centre was a square plate of the same material and it bore the initials IHS. The entire item was fixed with small screws to a cross of the crucifix type with its arms and legs supporting the whole design. The arms and upright of the cross comprised bars of metal about a third of an inch thick.

I saw that the top and bottom tips of the cross's upright each had a hole drilled through them. The whole thing was rather dirty with earth and green mould and I guessed some-one had scrubbed it in an effort to clean it. I picked it up and weighed it in the palm of my hand to find it was quite heavy and I must admit I thought it was brass, not gold. And the initials IHS were also familiar to me.

They appeared on many Catholic objects although the letters came from the Greek IHC which in turn came from the Greek spelling of Christ's name (IHCOYC). When that abbreviation was translated into Latin around the fif-teenth century, the letters appeared as IHS. This later came to mean Iesus, Hominum Salvator. Iesus referred to Jesus and Hominum Salvator meant Saviour of Mankind thus the familiar letters IHS mean Jesus, Saviour of Mankind, now shown as Humankind.

'It seems that this object is something with a religious meaning or symbolism,' I explained. 'It reminds me of the monstrance used in Benediction in the Catholic Church,' and I gave my reasons as I described a monstrance to him. It is a decorative container for the Sacred Host and it stands on the altar. It looks rather similar to the object I was holding, except this one did not have a base of any kind so it would never stand erect. It would have to be screwed onto a support of some kind.

'So this would fit in with the idea that this might have been a tithe barn,' he smiled. 'Something religious, especially with a former priory nearby?'

'And we must not forget the name of this building,' I added for good measure. 'Salutation. The name appears on lots of old inns that were formerly monastic hostels used by pilgrims, others include the Seven Stars, The Star, Angel, Ark, Mitre and so on.'

'So by establishing just what this object is, and its age or symbolism, we might discover something about the history of my new home and studio?'

'That's quite possible,' was all I could promise.

'So do you think it is gold?' was his next question.

'I doubt it,' I had to be honest. 'It looks rather like brass, especially with its discolouration, but we would need an expert opinion.'

'Do I do that, or do you?'

'If you're reporting this to me as a possible piece from a treasure trove, then I can do it for you. But for it to qualify as treasure trove, it must be either gold or silver, and it must have been deliberately hidden.'

'It was in a hole in the wall,' he told me. 'Over there.'

'Hidden, do you think?'

'Put there for safe keeping maybe. I can't really be sure why it was there.'

'Right, I'll treat it as a prospective treasure trove which means I can take it away and have it expertly assessed so that the coroner can decide whether or not to hold an inquest. If it is gold, he will do that to determine whether it was deliberately hidden or just stored for safety: if it was stored for safety, or if it is only brass, it will be returned to you, if he does declare it treasure trove, it will be surrendered to the state, but you will be paid the full commercial value.'

'Seems fair enough,' was his response so I gave him a receipt for the object and said I would take it immediately to a jeweller in Ashfordly to have it assessed and inform him of the outcome. I explained to Mr Carson I hoped to return to him later that same day.

I left and drove immediately to Ashfordly where I took the object to Selbourne and Hobson who were top class jewellers. Mr Adrian Selbourne, a silver-haired man in his sixties, had previously examined objects that were the subject of inquests, and furthermore, he had expert knowledge of the history of the locality. He was at the counter when I entered his shop.

'Ah, PC Rhea, not another piece of possible gold or silver, is it?' he smiled as I began to release the item from Mr Carson's wrapping of brown paper.

'I doubt it.' Once it was free, I passed it to him. 'I think it's brass.'

For his preliminary examination, he took it and examined it closely, weighing it in his hands, tapping it, lightly scratching it with his finger nail and then placing it on some scales. 'Hmmm,' he repeated several times. 'Very interesting.'

Then he said, 'Sorry, Mr Rhea, but I do not need to go further with this one, no need for the acid test, as they say. This is neither gold nor indeed bronze, it is brass as you thought, of that there is no doubt, but I suspect it is quite ancient. Possibly from the fifteenth century. And brass cannot be treasure trove. Have you any idea what it is?'

'It could be something with a religious background, it reminds me of the monstrance used in Catholic churches,' was all I could suggest. 'And it has some religious writing on it.'

'Hmmm,' he nodded. 'That makes sense. Yes, it is a religious artefact, PC Rhea, the initials IHS confirm that, but I doubt you'd find one on an altar, even in medieval times. So tell me, where has it come from?'

'It's from a remote building in High Rannockdale, very isolated. A man is converting it into a modern house and recording studio. It's called Salutation. He found it tucked into a hole in one of his walls, probably put there for safe keeping.'

'Ah, yes, I know the place. So Salutation's going to be occupied after all this time?'

'He's got a lot of work ahead of him, it'll take years,' I ventured. 'I was intrigued by the place and its name. It's just "Salutation", nothing else.'

'I think, in centuries gone by, it was a tithe barn, Mr Rhea, but in more recent times—and we are still talking of centuries ago—it was used as a hearse house. It would double as a sort of unofficial local mortuary or chapel of rest.'

'Really? Right out there in the middle of nowhere?'

'When someone died in a tiny house in any of the villages around those moors, the deceased could not be kept in the family bedroom, and in those times coffins were not used at funerals. People were buried in shrouds, perhaps wool or linen. Rich people could afford to pay for smart coffins, but for the poor there was a parish coffin that was available to all. This would come along in the hearse to collect the corpse soon after death. The deceased was placed in it and taken away to the hearse house and kept there until the date of the funeral which could be after a considerable time. It was a long way from any village, but in fact served several local communities and the lonely farms up there. There might even be several bodies without coffins awaiting burial at any one time, and each village had its own horse-drawn hearse—hence that very large building. Then on the day of the funeral the hearse returned to the house of the deceased with the body so that a formal funeral procession could be created. That's how things were done on our moors out of necessity, I'm not sure whether similar procedures applied elsewhere. Probably not.'

'So lots of local folks used that place on the moors? Salutation?'

'Indeed they did.'

'So why that odd name?'

'Down the centuries, PC Rhea, people would salute a passing coffin, probably a relic of the days when they were Catholics and made the sign of the cross. So in this case, centuries ago, when people passed that old hearse house, they would salute it just in case a body or even several bodies were stored there.'

'And so it became known as Salutation. It's a nicer name than the hearse house. But what puzzled me,' I admitted, 'was why was there just one word in the name?'

'I think the surrounding area—that expanse of moor-land—is also known as Salutation. At one stage, the route past the old hearse house was very busy with horse and foot traffic, but now it is rarely used. The old road is too rough for cars, but there's always speculation about surfacing it to cope with modern traffic.'

'Thanks for explaining all that, it's made my job easier.'

'I think the history of Mr Carson's building explains this curious item, PC Rhea. It is a piece of coffin furnishing. Someone would make these and they would be screwed onto the coffin lid before the procession. So now you have something to tell your friend at Salutation.'

'I have to ask this on his behalf—is it valuable?'

'I'd say it is not worth much and would hesitate to put a price on it. But to an expert in funereal artefacts, it might be a highly prized collectors' item. After all, there are not many of them around—most would have been buried centuries ago.'

And so I returned to Mr Carson at Salutation and gave him the news.

'I might keep it and have it screwed onto my coffin,' he smiled. 'But thanks for getting it sorted out. And the offer of a meal still stands!'

I told him I was soon to be transferred to a new post and wished him well with his house renovation and musical career. Several years later, the house and studio were finished and occupied and although I drove past on a road that had since been surfaced, I did not call. It was hardly polite to do so because my car was full of my family and I was not sure whether Mr Carson still lived there.

But I did notice a large sign displayed at one end of Salutation that said, 'Salutation Recording Studio.'

That was a name that meant something!

CHAPTER 5

Even as late as the 1960s—the era in which I was the village constable at Aidensfield—many local people, especially those living in isolated areas, rarely locked the doors of their homes or outbuildings. One reason given was that 'there's nowt worth pinching,' another was trust in one's neighbours and visitors, and the third may have been the effects of the law on burglary. Until 1968 that crime carried a maximum sentence of life imprisonment, a good deterrent even if it was rarely, if ever, imposed. Burglary, which until that year involved breaking into someone's house at night, was clearly regarded as a very serious crime. Indeed, it had earlier ranked alongside murder when it formerly carried the death penalty.

In 1968, however, the status of burglary was reduced to something akin to housebreaking that was a far less serious offence. The 'new' crime of burglary was committed when someone entered any building as a trespasser at any time of the day with the intention of stealing or committing other specified crimes. At this time—and subsequently—the means by which a householder could defend his or her property was also being questioned. For example, could a person use force against an intruder in the family home? If so, how much force could they use? How could such force be quantified if it occurred in the heat of the moment?

Here I quote from p.910 of *Archbold's Criminal Pleading, Evidence and Practice (1949)*, published by Sweet and Maxwell. The paragraph reads:

> *In defence of a man's house, the owner and his family may kill a trespasser who would forcibly dispossess him of it, in the same manner he might, by law, kill in self-defence a man who attacks him personally: with this distinction, however, that in defending his house he need not retreat as in other cases of self-defence for that would be giving up his house to his adversary.*

The references are: 1 Hale 485,468; R v Hussey 89 JP 28; 41 TLR 205; 18 Cr.App.R.160. In referring to this, I am reminded of a very ancient case where an elderly gentleman's house was entered at night by a team of seven burglars but he was equal to the occasion because he took up his sword and slaughtered the lot. For that action he was awarded a knighthood, but sadly I cannot recall the man's name or the year of the case. Certainly the story is contained in an old law book, but since that time, the means by which we can protect our home has been greatly reduced. The official line is that we can use such force as is reasonable in the circumstances—but what is 'reasonable' if one's home, life and precious belongings are under attack?

There can be no doubt such changes now mean that an Englishman's home can no longer be regarded as his impregnable castle. Those ancient laws indicated that one's home was inviolate and for that reason the lawful right to defend it had long been vigorously protected. It might be argued that such protection has since been seriously eroded.

Despite changes to the law and to legal procedures, the householders and farmers of Aidensfield and district were unimpressed. The law and police crime-prevention advice seemed to have little relevance to their lives and so they left open their doors and windows during their absence or when in bed. Not surprisingly in later years, some found themselves targets of determined and skilful thieves. Several of the attacked premises were very close to Ashfordly and Aidensfield but there was evidence that the thieves were not local people. They came from afar by using vehicles which were proving to be highly efficient aids for criminals.

As an example, the villains would drive to an isolated farm when the farmer and his wife were known to be at market, steal whatever they wanted and be miles away or even have disposed of identifiable property before the crime was discovered. That made detection very difficult, while the fact that the criminals crossed police boundaries to carry out their crimes in different police areas added to the problem.

In some cases it took a long time for the police to realize there was a pattern to such crimes simply because they occurred over such a wide area within a variety of police force areas. At that time, the national or regional criminal intelligence systems were not very well developed and so a series of thefts in, say, an area of the East Riding Constabulary might not be known to officers in the North Riding even though the scenes of crime might be only some five or ten miles apart. Furthermore, individual cases often occurred after a gap of weeks or even months and were therefore dealt with by different officers. There was no continuity. Had they all been attended by the same police officer, he would probably have noticed a trend or connection—sadly this did not happen in many cases.

I became aware of this tendency when a crime occurred on my beat one Thursday in April. I learned about it on the following Friday morning when I received a phone call from a farmer called Jacob Atkinson who lived at Moor End Farm, Briggsby. It was nearly half-past ten in the morning when he rang and fortunately I was at home dealing with some paperwork in my office.

'Now then, Mr Rhea, thoo'll have to get thisself here sharpish, we've been burgled.'

'What's gone, Mr Atkinson?'

'A load o' money, that's what. Our savings.'

'How much?'

'Now it's no good you asking me that, we just stuffed our spare cash into a milk churn and left it there . . .'

'Left it where?'

'In t'larder.'

'Where did they break in?'

'Break in? Nay, lad, they just walked in. We never lock up, there's never been t'need to lock up.'

'There is a need now, Mr Atkinson, there're more criminals about and they're using cars to travel far and wide. But let's concentrate on your crime for just a moment. When did it happen?'

'Yesterday, I think, Mr Rhea, but we didn't notice it until this morning.'

'Do you know if anyone saw anything? Cars? People? I need descriptions, car numbers and so on.'

'Nobody saw nowt, Mr Rhea, 'cos we weren't 'ere, and as thoo knows we're a mile from t'main road. We've no neighbours within a mile or two.'

'Right, don't touch anything, we'll probably need our fingerprinting officers and a Scene of Crime team to come and examine the area. I'll advise you about that when I see you. I'll be there in fifteen minutes.'

From my office I rang Ashfordly Police Station to inform Alf Ventress of my intended destination and the reason for my journey.

'No more reports of Greengrass at large on his "dog cart", Nick,' he informed me. 'Or that puma. I reckon folks have been seeing things. Maybe no puma and no "dog cart" after all? People can be mistaken, can't they? It'll be UFOs next!'

'Indeed they can, Alf, but I'll keep my ears and eyes open, just in case.'

My journey to Moor End Farm took a mere fifteen minutes with the final mile being over a rough, unsurfaced track full of ruts and pot-holes and marked by two closed gates.

I felt sure I would dislodge the exhaust pipe on one of the bumps but the little van rattled and groaned onwards until I reached the farmyard.

This was the route used by the raiders! They must have had advance knowledge of the prize that awaited them! In negotiating the lane, I wondered whether they had left any evidence. Tyre marks perhaps? Footprints near the gates? A discarded exhaust pipe or some other vehicle part? But they'd left nothing because the ground was dry and hardened like rock and I found nothing that might have fallen from their vehicle.

When I arrived in the farmyard, hens were running free with some pecking on a heap of fresh manure while a pair of pigs grunted and approached my van. I wondered if they were expecting food but they trotted off when I parked and switched off the engine. I made for the kitchen door doing my best not to stand in something nasty. Mrs Atkinson—Helen—noticed my approach and opened the door before I arrived, calling, 'Come in, Mr Rhea, you'll have a piece of pie and a mug of tea.'

'Well, it's not long since my breakfast . . .' I began my modest protest.

'Not to worry, there's always plenty here. Come in and sit down, then I'll fetch Jacob.'

In her early seventies with red cheeks and iron-grey hair, she was wearing a flowered apron and black boots, almost the working uniform of a moorland farmer's wife. She was a very large woman with heavy lips and jowls and she stomped everywhere rather like the Goliath who tried to slay David. I wondered what she might have done to the thieves if she had caught them. Would she have belaboured them with a rolling pin? I would have hoped so! However, I obeyed her invitation and settled at the circular kitchen table that was laden with pies and cakes, wondering if she'd been expecting the entire police force. A cat came in and peered up at me, then decided I had nothing to offer so it wandered away and disappeared into the interior of the farmhouse. Then I heard voices and footsteps.

'Now then, Mr Rhea,' smiled Jacob as he came in behind Helen with muck on his feet because he'd been milking. Approaching seventy-five, I reckoned, he was a heavily-built man with a happy weathered face and a no-nonsense manner. He discarded his heavy corduroy jacket and hung it on the back of a chair. 'You got here then.'

'Not for the first time,' I responded with a chuckle. 'Once a quarter to check your stock registers is enough for any little van coming along that lane of yours. I'm surprised your vehicles have any under-parts left.'

'Aye, well, there's a lot o' life in t'lane yet, it's got a good thick base o' rock and stuff, there's no need for t'expense of putting tarmac down and you can allus repair cars and trucks. But it's a rum do when you can't leave your own house without some bastards coming to nick all your savings. What do you make o' that?' and he sat down beside me with a huge sigh and helped himself to a mug of tea and pork pie. Helen then joined us. I opened my notebook and placed it on the table as I waited until they were settled down then asked,

'So tell me all about it. When did the thieves break in?'

I did not use the term 'burglars' because this crime appeared to have happened during the daytime, but even at that time by opening an unlocked door with malicious intent, it would be classified as a break-in but not burglary. It was a legal technicality but on the face of things, the crime was housebreaking.

'They didn't break in, Mr Rhea, as I said on t'phone. They just walked in and helped themselves.' Jacob was acting as spokesman.

'So where were you? Both of you? Down the fields? In the outhouses?'

'Nay, lad, it's Eltering Livestock Mart on Thursdays. We were there. All day. Left here at seven with a load o' beasts, sold 'em at a profit, stayed on to see what's what and got back here at five or summat like that. We didn't notice owt wrong until this morning. Helen went to put our profit away and saw t' churn had been nicked.'

'Churn?'

'Aye, we keep our cash in a milk churn, in t'larder. Like lots o' farmers do. You need a fair supply of cash on hand at times. You can't do a proper deal wi' promises, you need cash on hand.'

'Right, I get the picture. So clearly the thieves knew you were out,' was my first comment. 'This house is a long way from the road, they couldn't have noticed it was unoccupied simply by driving past because it can't be seen from the road. They wouldn't risk coming all this way down your lane and being seen if they were up to no good. I reckon they knew you were out, and knew what they would find when they got here.'

'How would they know that?'

'I don't know, I was hoping you might tell me.'

'Aye, Ah've been wondering about that, Mr Rhea, getting my thinking-cap on. Mebbe they sat watching for when we left? Mind you, we never saw anybody watching us though. No strangers about in our fields or parked on t'road outside.'

'Let's look at it from another angle, Jacob. Maybe they knew you were regulars at the mart? Did anyone know you went to mart every Thursday? Or that you kept money in a milk churn? Have you ever seen anyone hanging about near your lane end on other mart days? Or at any time? Watching for you leaving?'

'No, not a soul, Mr Rhea but most local farmers know we go to mart, they all do.'

'It's clear that somebody else knows, Jacob.'

As we chatted, we were enjoying the pies, cakes and tea. I paused a moment in an attempt to sort out in my own mind whether or not a crime had actually been committed. It seemed a rather unlikely scenario here, but I had come across people who had concealed their savings and then forgotten where they had put them, only to report them stolen when they could not be found. I knew one old lady who concealed her £1 notes and fivers in the hearth, hiding them among the paper she used to light the fire. Then one autumn day she lit her fire after an absence during the summer and a hundred pounds or more went up in smoke. Another farmer had concealed his paper money savings in a hole inside the chimney and when he went for it, it had turned into powder due to the constant heat. In this case with no sign of a break-in there were already the elements of such an attempt to hide money. But I had to continue and one important task was to examine the scene.

'So where did they get in?'

'Same door as you, I expect. It's allus unlocked.'

'Any sign of footprints, dirt, dropped mud, that sort of thing?'

'Nowt,' said Helen. 'We've had a few dry days. You'd never know anybody had been in. T'door was shut when we got back.'

'And you are absolutely sure somebody has been into the house and stolen your money?'

'Not only that, Mr Rhea,' confirmed Jacob. 'They've taken t'milk churn an' all. It was one of my best 'uns, good milk churns aren't easy to come by in these modern times, they don't make 'em like they used to. Ah've had yon churn for years and years.'

'They have your farm name on, don't they? The churns I mean.'

'Oh, aye, Moor End Briggsby on t'lid and sides, in red paint. They've a pair o' strong handles an' all. That's so as t'milk lorry driver knows where to leave 'em when they're emptied and can lift 'em when they're full, and not get 'em mixed up with other folk's churns. And we can't do with having other folk's churns on our stands, it would confuse things, believe me.'

'Well, the name on it will help if we find it abandoned somewhere.'

'You'll not find it around here; they'd need it to carry all t'cash. Either that or a wheelbarrow.'

'Good grief!' I exclaimed. 'You mean it was actually full of money?'

'Aye, cash and notes. It would take two of 'em to lift it.'

'Would it be that heavy?' I began to realize this was no ordinary money box!

'Oh, aye, it was full o' pennies, ha'pennies, three-penny bits, tanners, bobs, half-crowns and a lot o' notes, ten bob notes, pound notes and mebbe even a fiver or two. All packed in tight. Stuffed well down over t'years.'

'So how much money are we talking about?'

'Now that's summat I wouldn't actually know, Mr Rhea. We never get round to counting it.'

'But surely you must have some idea.'

'Well, there was this chap who took his milk churn full o' money to t'bank to pay it in and he reckoned it held about £5,000 . . . but when t' bank chap counted it there was only £4,900. He'd taken t'wrong churn, you see . . .' and he chuckled. 'By gum, that's a tale that does t'rounds, Mr Rhea. Ah've heard it many times but I reckon it's true. There's a few farmers like that around these parts.'

'So you're saying *your* churn might have contained about £5,000?'

'Summat like that, Mr Rhea. Spare cash. It all adds up over time and we've been filling yon churn for years and years. I don't trust banks or tax men or accountants or folks like that, so I keep my own money handy in case I want some in a rush, to buy new cattle, pigs or sheep or summat. Mebbe a tractor or a binder.'

For me at that time, £5,000 was more than six years' wages; £600 would buy a good new car and a lot of houses would cost less than £5,000. If this was true it was a huge sum to lose. There was no doubt someone knew it was here for the taking.

'It seems to me that somebody knew you kept it in the house and also knew you'd be out all day yesterday. It would take some time to get here, lift the heavy churn and then leave without being seen.' They were obvious remarks, but I had to stress these points in case it produced a memory from either husband or wife.

'Aye, I expect that's 'ow it 'appened.'

'You'd better show me where it went from.' I was still struggling to come to terms with the unlikely story they were telling me, but I also had to take heed of the scale of this theft. I wondered whether the Atkinsons were insured for such a crime—it was not easy to insure for the theft of cash. Maybe the churn was covered? As I pondered these curious facts, Mr and Mrs Atkinson led me into the larder at the back of the kitchen. The door was standing open and like all larders in moorland farms and houses, it was at the rear of the house with the outer wall facing north to ensure it was cool throughout the year. There was a solid stone cool shelf to accommodate perishables, such as eggs, cheese and milk, and a tiny glass window covered with a narrow mesh to keep out flies and other insects. Under the cool shelf there were two milk churns. I noticed there was space for a third with just a hint of a ring mark on the floor—but that space was empty.

'There, Mr Rhea, yon space. That's where it went from. It was there yesterday morning sure as eggs is eggs.'

'Would the larder door be open, like it is now?'

'Shut more than likely, but just a push will open it.'

'So it was not locked either? They wouldn't have to break it open?'

'Nowt like that, it needs to be loose so as t'missus can push her way in wi' hands full o' baking or trays or whatever.'

'So you are telling me, Jacob, that somebody drove all that way down your lane and crept into your house yesterday while you were at the livestock mart, coming in through an outer door that wasn't locked, and then through this door that wasn't locked either, and carried off that churn which you say was heavy enough to require two men to lift it? And it probably contained something like £5,000?'

'Aye, that's about it, Mr Rhea. I couldn't lift it by myself. You might know, Mr Rhea, that £1's worth of pennies, that's 240 of 'em, weigh summat like two and a half pounds but not all the stuff in that churn was pennies. So I don't know what it would weigh, except that it would be too much for one feller to carry on his own. All t'coins sink to t'bottom over time, sliding off t'notes, a bit like gravel settling. Put a half-crown on t'top of a pile of banknotes in t'churn and it'll be gone next day, sunk out o' sight, sliding its way day by day right to t'bottom.'

'I follow. So is any of the money marked so you'd recognize it? Initials on the bank notes for example? Dabs of colour on notes with larger denominations?'

'Marked? There's never been a need to mark money, Mr Rhea.'

'There is if we want to catch someone in possession of your cash, we need to be certain any money we recover is actually yours. The thieves could say they got it from anywhere, change in a pub, out of the bank, winnings at the races, a deal of some sort . . .'

'Well, t'churn's mine, that's all I can say. And like I said, it's marked even if nowt else is.'

'Let's think about the feasibility of shifting that churn. How heavy do you think it would be? I'm thinking in general terms—how heavy would any churn be if it was full of coins and notes?'

'Depends how many coins there are, Mr Rhea, but as a rough guide, bearing in mind our own experiences, I'd say heavier than two sacks o' taties or a bags o' cattle feed but not as heavy as a full cart load o' taties.'

'And how much is that?'

'A couple of hundredweight mebbe or a bit more, depending on how much was coins and how much was notes. Here, you can try to lift one of these others to see what I mean.'

And he pointed to the pair of churns under the cool shelf.

'What's in these?' I asked.

'Money,' he said.

'More money?' I was aghast at this. 'Good grief, Jacob, how much have you got stored in here?'

'Summat like twice as much as that 'un that's gone,' he shrugged his shoulders. 'Mebbe £5,000 in each one, but that's just a guess.'

I lifted the lid of the nearest and it was packed full of notes—as Jacob had told me, the coins had apparently sunk to the bottom by sliding between the notes.

When I tried to lift it, it was impossible. I could budge it very slightly by tipping it to one side but nothing more. And the second one was exactly the same—full of coins and notes.

'Are you sure one's gone missing?' I had to ask the obvious question.

'Oh aye, there's no doubt about it, Mr Rhea. There was three when we left home yesterday morning. You can see where it stood on t'floor.'

He was right. The circular mark on the stone floor was good evidence of that.

'Now, let's think about this. Could the churn have been stolen last night? When you were in bed?'

'Nay, Mr Rhea, we'd 'ave 'eard 'em shifting it, seen t'lights o' their car or van or whatever. And we'd 'ave 'eard t'noise. And our geese would 'ave made a racket, not to mention t'dogs barking.'

The crime was clearly not a burglary, but it was a serious crime, nonetheless. I continued, 'So the churn that's gone, is that your most recent one or an older one?'

'That's t'oldest, Mr Rhea, that 'un that's gone. We're putting our cash into this 'un now,' and he indicated the one nearest the door. 'I'd say that 'un that's gone is our oldest and we've been filling it for years, mebbe for fifty years or summat like, since we got married that will be.'

'Fifty years? So there'll be some very old notes and coins in there?'

'Oh, aye. Sometimes I've had to chuck old notes out when they've gone mouldy, that larder can be very damp at times. I've seen notes black with mould and coins all green wi' t'dampness. Burning t'rotten old notes is t'best way o' getting rid of 'em. You could catch summat from 'em.'

'So you don't take them to the bank to get them changed for good ones? They will do that, you know.'

'Ah've never had owt to do with banks, Mr Rhea. We allus keep our cash in here, where we know where it is and where we can keep an eye on it.'

'Well, Jacob, think hard about this—now you've had thieves in the house, they'll know there's other churns full of money, won't they?'

'You're saying they might be back?'

'I think that's a very strong possibility if they looked under those lids. Clearly, they didn't have time to delay things while they struggled with three churns, they might have had trouble managing just one. So Jacob and Helen, can I suggest you put the contents of these two churns into a bank for safe keeping?'

'Hide 'em, more like,' he said. 'And give them villains a backside full of lead shot if they come again.'

At that stage, I was beginning to wonder how my superiors would react when I submitted my crime report—they would not believe what they were reading and would probably suspect some kind of insurance fiddle by Jacob Atkinson. I had to make the story seem infinitely more sensible while not detracting in any way from the seriousness of his loss.

'Are you insured against burglaries and housebreaking?' I asked.

'Nay, Mr Rhea, not us. There's never been a need.'

I wanted to sit down for a few minutes to consider my next course of action and so I moved out of the cramped larder and back into the kitchen where Helen refilled my mug with tea and offered me another bun, a chocolate one on a plate. As I sat in momentary silence I could feel the eyes of Mr and Mrs Atkinson upon me, expecting me to do something positive. It was rather like having a couple of spaniels looking at me, willing me to take them for a walk.

The snag was it was very unlikely we would recover the cash—cash was so easy to dispose of and there was no way I could link that unknown amount of money with the Atkinsons. Furthermore, the thieves probably had a full day's start on us. I felt the only hope was the missing milk churn.

With his farm name painted upon it, it might be recovered if it had been dumped somewhere once it was empty, or else someone might have noted a vehicle approaching the farm after the couple had gone to market.

The churn could also bear the fingerprints of the thieves. That could be very important. And, of course, both Mr and Mrs Atkinson might recall whether or not they had revealed their address and regular absences to anyone attending Eltering Mart. So there was plenty of positive work ahead and I prayed that luck might be shining down upon us.

But perhaps the most worrying aspect was the presence of two more churns full of cash—sure as eggs are eggs, the villains would return for one of them and then another even at widely differing times. My personal view was that we should set a trap and arrange a reception committee for them—preferably without Jacob's shotgun. Without advance knowledge, selecting the right dates would be difficult.

'I've been thinking,' I said. 'There are several courses of action I could take.'

I explained that it would be wise for the Scenes of Crime officers and fingerprint experts to visit the scene as early as possible, preferably later today if they weren't committed with other jobs. Their skills could be useful even though there was apparently very little evidence of the raid. I explained that the officers were highly skilled and might find something invisible to the naked eye, even a footprint outside, a tyre-mark, fingerprint, hair or piece of fibre from the thieves' clothing.

We needed something to link the offenders to the scene if and when they were traced. If the churn was found discarded somewhere, it would surely bear fingerprints or some other kind of evidence—that churn could be crucial. I repeated my advice that the couple should place their savings in a bank and offered to introduce them to my own bank manager after they had considered the matter. But of more immediate importance was to protect the couple against a repeat visit by setting a trap with empty churns, or churns full of fake or marked notes.

I explained that I and my colleagues would make enquiries at Eltering Mart and at other markets in the area with a view to tracing the culprits, possibly through other victims, but I stressed that Mr and Mrs Atkinson must do a little investigating of their own. They would surely be aware of who, at the mart, either staff or customers, would know about their weekly visits and their hoard of cash. They promised to help in any way they could.

All that Mr Atkinson would say was that, 'Everybody at yon mart is there at t'same time, Mr Rhea, all on a Thursday and all buying and selling. Leaving their farms empty. Folks come and go—we've allus trusted each other, till now. Now I don't know who to trust.'

'Don't forget a member of staff might be involved, even tipping off his accessories when he could see you were at the mart, and so he'd know your farm would be deserted at the time. And try to think who knew you kept your money in those churns.'

'Aye, I'll do that but it is summat of a worry, thinking folks are out there watching and waiting to rob us.'

'I agree. It is a worry. But remember the villains might not be members of the farming community, they could be professional thieves from somewhere like Hull, Middlesbrough, Leeds or Scarborough, you might not be their only victims. Get your neighbours and friends talking about the raids.'

'Oh, aye, that makes sense, Mr Rhea. I'd allus trust my mates and neighbours. Not strangers though.'

Now that I had set his mind working towards a solution and also towards safeguarding his remaining savings, I was increasingly concerned that the money left in the remaining two churns would be a great temptation. Did the thieves know exactly what was inside them? Would they have looked inside or would they have been too keen to get away before attracting attention? Another and worse scenario was that they might even return to the house when it was occupied and use violence if there was any resistance. After all, there was a lot of money at stake. If they did return, I hoped it would be when there was a reception committee, not Jacob with his shotgun but a police officer or two.

'Why don't I take you to the bank in Ashfordly now?' I suggested before leaving. 'My bank will be open. We could take those churns in my van and I could introduce you to the manager who'll look after your cash . . .'

'Aye, but if I put my cash in there,' he frowned, 'I'll never get it back, I'll get some other bugger's money instead of my own . . .'

'Well, yes, that's how the system works, you don't get your own actual cash back if you draw money out.'

'But I allus like to have my hands on my own money, Mr Rhea.'

'Banks don't work like that,' I could see he was having difficulty understanding how the bank system operated, then I had a bright idea.

'One alternative, Jacob, is a safe deposit box where you can leave your own valuables under lock and key, with only you having access. No one would know what was being kept there and if it was cash, then you'd get your own coins and notes back whenever you wanted.'

'Now that sounds a bit more like it, Mr Rhea. Aye, I'm right pleased you told me that. So if I do that, them fellers might come again and get nowt? Except a backside full o' lead pellets.'

'Right,' I was hopeful now. 'Your money would always be safe because you'd have the key and no one else, not even the bank manager, could touch it. But you could only get access during the bank's opening hours.'

'What do you think to that, our Helen?'

'I think it's very sensible idea, Jacob. You've a lot to thank Mr Rhea for.'

'Right, Mr Rhea. Let's do it.'

Instead of me placing the churns in the rear of the police van, he decided he would ferry them to the bank in Ashfordly on the trailer behind his tractor because he had another job to do in town. Helen decided not to come and join us as she had things to do. Besides, earning and caring for money was considered man's work. That suited me because I could call in at Ashfordly Police Station to complete my initial crime report and arrange for the Scenes of Crime and Fingerprints teams to visit Moor End Farm as soon as possible. I could also set in motion the plans to ambush the thieves should they ever return. It required the pair of us to lift the churns out of the house and onto the trailer where they looked just like a pair of ordinary milk churns being carried on farm business. No one would ever realize what they contained.

And so it was that the little procession left Moor End Farm along its bumpy and unsurfaced road and less than ten minutes later we were easing into the bank's car park. I told Jacob I would go ahead of him to alert the manager to the task awaiting him.

'You're not going to believe this, John,' I told the manager as we settled in his office. 'But I've got a chap out there with two milk churns full of money that he wants to put into a safe deposit . . .'

'This isn't an April Fool's joke is it?' he laughed. 'That yarn is one of the classic Yorkshire banking stories. We all know the tale about the farmer and his milk churns, about his wife bringing the wrong one that had only four thousand pounds and a bit more inside, instead of fetching the one containing five thousand.'

'No, this is genuine,' and I explained about the theft and the two remaining churns—and Jacob's reluctance to deal with banks.

'There's nothing new in that,' smiled John Hammond. 'There're lots of old folks out there who have no idea how banks work and an amazing number who still can't get to grips with the idea of using cheques instead of cash. Anyway, thanks for putting him in touch with me, I'll have a word with him.'

After making the introductions I could see that Jacob was surprisingly nervous, but after we had helped him to carry the heavy churns into the bank manager's personal office, we were shown the vaults containing the safe deposit boxes and Jacob was delighted to see there were some were large enough to accommodate his pair of churns.

'If you want to take your churns home,' suggested John, 'we have secure boxes you can use. And, Mr Atkinson, we don't need to count the cash because we do not want to know what your safe contains. Only you will know that.'

'But it'll cost summat, will it? To use this spot?'

'Yes, it is a service we offer so there is a small charge.'

'Well, it costs me nowt to store these in my larder, Mr Hammond.'

'But you've lost a churn worth a few pounds along with about £5,000 worth of cash. That wouldn't happen here. Anyway, you could put some of your money into a deposit account with us and that would earn interest which in turn would pay the fees.'

'Earn interest, what's that mean?'

'It means if you put your money into a deposit account with us but not in this safe, we would pay you something in return. That would pay for this safe deposit. Your money would keep working for you and provide an income, then we can open a current account so that you would have a cheque book you could use to pay your bills. You could buy and sell livestock or equipment without using cash.'

'Aye, I've heard about cheques, some of the chaps and dealers at the mart use 'em, but they nowt but paper, they're not real money. Real money's important to me, Mr Hammond.'

'I think it's time I went to my office,' I interrupted. 'And Jacob, you can trust John, he'll give you good advice while explaining how the banking system works, and you can rest assured your money will be safe here. Now I've work to do, I must talk to our CID and set about trying to find your missing churn and its load.'

'Aye, right, well, thanks Mr Rhea.'

'Right, I'll be off. I'll be in touch as soon as I have news. I might call in on my way home today just to see how you're getting on. And you will get a visit from our Scenes of Crime officers. Together we'll do our best to find your money.'

'And my churn?'

'Yes, and your churn.'

When I arrived at Ashfordly Police Station, the sergeant had gone to Eltering for a sub-divisional meeting but Alf Ventress was on duty in the office. I explained events at Moor End Farm whereupon he said,

'That's very odd, Nick. A circular came only this morning from the Regional Crime Squad. There have been lots of raids at isolated farms in recent weeks and their boss is seeking more information about cases that have happened in our area. I'll send a note about Moor End Farm and will put the idea of a trap to him. They've not all had milk churns nicked though! Several have resulted in antiques and jewellery being taken, but the common factor is they've all occurred at isolated farms on market days, not all of which had unlocked doors. There were some break-ins. I'll make sure Scenes of Crime attend with a fingerprint expert. They'll ring the Atkinsons before they make a definite date or time.'

In that way, the routine response was put into action and it included a wide notification of the crime in local and regional circulars. I called upon the Atkinsons later that day to update them about the other cases and to remind them that police experts could soon be expected at their farm. I assured them I would continue my own enquiries and they promised to quiz their friends and contacts during their next visit to the cattle mart. And they would now lock their house before leaving it!

The Scenes of Crime officers and fingerprint experts found no useful evidence and so it looked as if the thieves had made a clean getaway with their loot, but then a few days later we had a stroke of good fortune.

A milk churn bearing the name Moor End Farm, Briggsby was found abandoned behind a hedge near Driffield in the East Riding and I received a call from the CID at Beverley.

One of their detectives had seen a reference to the raid in the regional Crime Information Newsletters and it was the curious theft of the milk churn that had attracted his attention. His name was Detective Constable Malcolm Collins. 'It looks like the churn from your crime,' he told me, 'but the odd thing is the contents are apparently intact.'

'Intact? All that money?' I asked.

'Well, it's not money now,' he laughed. 'All the old notes are rotten with damp and fungus; some are out-of-date and even the copper coins are covered with green mould while the silver money looks black and useless. I reckon our villains wanted rid of it, maybe they thought they would catch something nasty from it, foot-and-mouth or swine fever or some other animal disease! They are city types but in fact some of the cash could be used and the older rotten bits exchanged. They'd never risk that. So they ditched the churn and its contents.'

'So do you know who they are?'

'We do, their fingerprints were all over the churn. They're a couple of professional villains from Hull. We've been keeping tabs on them over the last few months. They raid isolated farms on market days and have recently been operating over a wider area, taking in parts of the North Riding as well as the East Riding and the Hull area, even down to Lincolnshire. We think they have a contact working inside the mart offices, probably some kind of freelance operator who visits all the marts and provides them with information about people who attend regularly and leave their premises deserted for the day. We're checking outgoing phone calls from all the local mart offices over the last year or so. That should help.'

'This is great news! Have you put this crime to them?'

'All in due course. The pair of them are inside now, helping the police with their enquiries, as we put it, thanks to that milk churn.'

'Will my farmer get it back?'

'All in good time. We'll get it back to him once we've finished with it from the scientific examination point of view and he might even get his money changed into proper cash.'

And so the story of Jacob's churns had a happy ending. The market insider informant was traced and so the three conspirators were dealt with and given a sentence of imprisonment while Jacob had his previous churn and most of his money restored. Some of it was beyond recognition. He had no idea whether any of his money was missing, but did promise that in future he would not store his life savings in milk churns. He'd use the bank.

'By gum, Mr Rhea,' he said after I broke the good news to him. 'Ah'm right glad you've found that churn of mine. It's a real good 'un, it's been in our family for years, ever since Ah was a lad. When Ah get it back Ah might keep it in that room Ah use as my office. Ah'll need somewhere to keep all my bank statements and cheque books, won't Ah?'

CHAPTER 6

As I prepared for my departure from Aidensfield, I checked the Greengrass Farm frequently at odd times, always with no sign of its notorious occupant and my enquiries into his whereabouts produced nothing. Apart from the few sightings already reported, no one else had spotted him touring the lanes with his "dog cart" and its husky or huskies. I kept Mrs Potiphar informed, but she admitted she had seen no more of our elusive character, neither had she received further reports of his "dog cart".

Likewise, I made enquiries about sightings of the puma and although several people had heard rumours of it, none had actually seen it and there were no reports of it attacking livestock or leaving a trail of any kind. One countryman told me that, if you wanted to hide something in a wood or even in the garden, you should paint it black. It would then merge with the shadows among undergrowth, trees or shrubs and so become almost invisible. The same man explained that it was not uncommon to find black foxes and even black fallow deer, but catching sight of them in woodland was nigh impossible. The reported puma could have been such a fox. The chances of seeing a puma, whatever its colour, roaming in the Yorkshire countryside were unlikely unless it showed itself in an open field or on the moors.

With no further reports on either of those projects, I continued my routine patrols. It was while serving at Aidensfield that it became clear village constables were expected to undertake tasks that formed no part of police work. This was the type of help expected from an available person whose responsibilities and skills were many and varied, and at times unspecific, like an odd-job man or a Jack-of-all-trades. I am sure many members of the public thought that police officers were there to help people in any manner possible and in any set of circumstances, irrespective of whether it was part of our duty.

Most police officers went along with that ideal and it is right to add that members of the public appreciated their police officers' work comprised rather more than catching people riding bikes without lights, shutting pub doors at closing time or helping old ladies to cross the road. The village bobby was widely regarded as a good Samaritan, a capable sort of character who was always available to deal with all those things that people could not cope with through their own efforts.

I did not mind tackling those miscellaneous chores because it meant the populace considered me approachable if they needed help of any sort. As their local constable, it meant my work was made easier because I knew they trusted me and weren't afraid to make a request, however unusual it might be.

Generally I was asked to assist with minor matters—I was never asked to fully decorate a house or service a car but I have helped to hang wallpaper, change a car's fan-belt or plugs, and a wheel with a punctured tyre. Some officers, male and female have suddenly found themselves assisting at the birth of a child or perhaps a calf, foal, puppies or lambs. Most of those extraneous tasks could be completed by anyone with a modicum of common sense and perhaps some useful physical strength. I did find it useful, however, to have basic skills with electric drills, hammers and screwdrivers, in addition to knowing how to change a fuse, unblock a drain or repair a dry-stone wall.

Times without number I helped drivers to start their cars on frosty mornings, pushing them as the owner sat in the driving seat with instructions to let in the clutch once a suitable speed had been achieved, hopefully while going downhill. Once when I was doing that, I was reminded of one farmer who always parked his car on top of the midden in winter because the heat rising from the rotting manure kept his engine warm and enabled his car to start with the minimum of trouble.

Like many other police officers I've helped children to re-fit chains to their pedal cycles, shown them how to mend punctures or even how to draw pictures of birds or cats. I've helped to fix defective toilet cisterns, put washers on dripping taps, painted woodwork or repaired door handles and I once helped a man in a loft to fix a switch in a bathroom below. That simple task needed two people, one in each room at the same time and I happened to be passing. Helping people to break into their own cars or homes when they had lost their keys was a common cry for help and on one occasion, I helped a man to drill a hole in a stone wall so that he could install an outside light. In his late fifties, he had never previously drilled a hole in a stone wall and had no idea how to either operate an electric drill or secure a screw in the hole, all of which I found astonishing.

Being born and reared in the countryside, I was taught from a very early age never to rely on others to effect routine tasks, maintenance and repairs. My dad fixed everything from cars to electrical objects via plumbing or wall-building—and he taught his children to do such things by themselves. This was long before DIY became a kind of cult—in our case it was always a case of necessity and certainly my contemporaries would never have comprehended paying anyone to fix a problem in the house or car, or to undertake tasks such as painting and decorating, fixing the lights, plumbing or coping with domestic emergencies.

Indeed, many countrymen and farmers were superb inventors and craftsmen who built their own devices to help in their work, some of which were amazingly clever and effective but never patented.

I remember that when I was first allocated a police house I was told I should not put a new washer on my own tap, fix a faulty ball-cock in a toilet cistern or paint my own front door because it was police property.

I and many of my colleagues could have saved the rate-payers a fortune by being allowed to undertake our own running repairs and maintenance. If I wanted a new washer on a dripping tap, for example, I had to make the request in triplicate and in writing and it would eventually be approved by an anonymous official at Force Headquarters before a plumber was commissioned to carry out the task at a cost of several pounds. It might take several days to get the problem fixed when I could have done the job myself in ten minutes at a cost of two pence for the washer. And I would not have claimed that two pence in expenses. The alternative—and costly—view was that many police officers were incapable of safely completing even a simple repair job, and there was always a risk of them causing damage or danger by their amateurish attempts. That accounts for all the red tape, bureaucracy and expense involved. I soon learned that such rules were necessary for the safety of both the tenant and the property and it must be said that some DIY practitioners were, and still are, notoriously inept. I must admit, though, I did fit a few tap washers and fix cisterns to save time and form-filling.

One fairly regular request was to 'print' letters for people who had to write to important people or official organizations. By asking me to 'print' the letters, what the person was really requesting was that I composed and typed them. The policeman was one of few people in the village who was accustomed to writing reports, was accessible to the public and who owned and used a typewriter. I was also asked to help people to complete a bewildering array of official forms, to sign passport applications and to witness signatures on wills and other formal documents.

Another frequent request was for me to speak to organizations such as the Catholic Women's League, Women's Institute, luncheon clubs, Rotary and Round Table or even parish council meetings.

Speaking to local organizations about my work was often considered part of my duty because it was a good public relations exercise on behalf of the Force. However there was immense danger in some cases, particularly when asked to judge competitions. The internal politics of some local organizations, clubs and groups had to be experienced to be believed.

On several occasions when I was a guest speaker at women's groups I was asked, 'Would you please judge tonight's competition?' Invariably I would answer in the positive without really knowing what I was letting myself in for, or what was expected of me and what pitfalls lay ahead. In many cases the competition might involve something I knew nothing about, such as knitting, lace making, crochet or making butterfly buns. In fact, a competition could involve anything from composing a piece of poetry to baking a cake or making a pie. There may be competitions involving photos of babies, paintings or sketches of parts of the village, a decorated egg or a wooden spoon dressed to look like a famous person. I've judged hats and scarves, gardens in tea cups or the best bunch of wild flowers picked that morning. Indeed, the competition at some monthly meetings could be absolutely anything but was usually something completely alien or incomprehensible to the average man.

Most organizations held their meetings in the evenings and they included the business session followed by the speaker and a light supper. The time for judging competitions had to somehow be squeezed in during those proceedings, hopefully when the audience—usually women—were chatting to one another during a break. Lots of them had a very frustrating habit of coming to talk to the judge while he or she was earnestly trying to reach a difficult decision of some kind. That made it almost impossible to concentrate on the task in hand. The trick was to complete one's judging when the attention of the audience was diverted but that was never easy.

The moment I went across to the table bearing the competition entries, I could guarantee a gaggle of women would join me to promptly tell me, for example, that Mrs Watkins always won with her poetry and that she shouldn't be allowed to win every time and that her poem tonight was not one of her best, or that it had won every time it had been exhibited so far—and it had appeared in every competition including the WI and the local Townswomen's Guild, not to mention other competitions in the village such as the annual garden fete or the church fair. That clever-clogs Annie Watkins had to be taken down a peg or two! Or so the audience suggested!

On all such occasions I did not know which of the entries had been written by the redoubtable Mrs Watkins and so it was inevitable that I awarded her yet another first prize because the poems were submitted anonymously. It was Sod's Law that her effort would be the best by far but some disgruntled losers would suggest in hoarse whispers that she had copied it from a volume written by a famous poet of bygone times. Wordsworth has a lot to answer for.

Quite often when I had finished my talk and was savouring my cup of tea and a bun, the president or competition secretary would confidentially advise me not to give first prize to the decorated egg on the left of the table because that had been done by Mrs Farquar. Mrs Farquar, I was told in a hoarse whisper, had won first prize with it last year and the year before that. But beyond doubt, the most difficult task was to judge the bonniest baby competition even if they were only photographs. Inevitably the audience consisted of proud and competitive mothers, aunts, grandmothers and even great grandmothers and I upset one group to whom I spoke by awarding all the babies equal first prize. In my opinion they all looked the same, all being junior editions of Winston Churchill. I felt that equal marks for all was a sensible solution but even that caused an almighty rumpus.

Judging baby contests is indeed a dangerous sport. Furthermore, there was no logic to many of those competitions—the best entry was not necessarily the worthiest of winners.

However, I can claim to have actually won such a competition. First prize was a silver teaspoon bearing the WI logo on its handle. It happened when my mother was asked to join her local branch and she did so with reluctance because she could not tolerate all the petty gossip, bitchiness and grumbles that inevitably surfaced at meetings. During her very short spell as a member—which lasted only a month or so—there was an Easter competition. It comprised the decoration of a hard-boiled egg and so Mum boiled hers but because she had absolutely no artistic ability, she asked me to decorate it. After some thought, I decided to paint the WI logo, which was oval and therefore egg-shaped, onto the side of her egg and so I did. It won first prize and Mum gave me that spoon. Was this cheating? I did know that some women won prizes with their husbands' best half-dozen plums, apples or tomatoes, or equally they won artistic or poetic competitions produced by their children or grandchildren or by a poet no one had discovered. I believe the rules for many such competitions did not state the work had to be actually completed by the competitor in person. Maybe those rules have now changed.

Some presidents, or chairmen as they were then called even if they were female, could be extremely ferocious and most unsympathetic to the needs of a speaker. On one occasion I drove sixty miles to deliver a talk and when I arrived, the entrance led directly into the hall where the audience was sitting and waiting. I desperately wanted to freshen up, have a drink of water and especially to go to the loo. But Madam President was having none of it.

'It's time for your talk, Mr Rhea, come along, don't waste time, we're all ready. We can't delay things; it's getting late and some of these people have buses to catch or have baby-sitters to take home.'

I had to think fast. 'I've left something in the car,' I said and rushed out to pee behind a bush growing near the rear wall of the hall. On another occasion, I drove about fifty miles from the North York Moors into the Yorkshire Dales and when a few miles from the venue of my talk, I discovered that a bridge across the river had been closed for repairs. To reach my destination involved a diversion of about twenty-six miles which meant I would be forty to forty-five minutes late for my talk. The ferocious president gave me an almighty dressing down before the gathering, saying how rude it was to be late. I stood meekly before her realizing I stood no chance in producing any kind of acceptable explanation in the force of her attack. However, as a prelude to my talk I gave a full account of my travels and bemoaned the fact no one had warned me the bridge was closed. But it did not make any difference—I was late and that was unforgivable as the president insisted on reminding me during the tea break. She even suggested I was ill-mannered by raising the matter before the audience! I was reminded of a lorry driver who stopped to ask a dalesman the way—'Do you know the Felldale turn-off?'

'Aye, I should do,' responded the dalesman, 'I married her.'

One of the funniest was the secretary of one organization who forgot to book me for a talk, even though she had reserved the date in her own diary. She realized her error the day before the engagement and on the actual day I received a letter from her that began, *Dear Mr Rhea. By a grave misfortune I should have asked you to speak to us on the 9th* . . . I didn't go, pleading another engagement.

The most memorable from my personal point of view was a request for me to speak to a Women's Institute meeting high in the Yorkshire Dales, the subject being 'The dialect of the North Riding'. This was a private engagement, not part of my police duty. The drive was nearly seventy miles from my then home in the North York Moors and I arrived early, hoping for some time to relax briefly before my talk. However when the president introduced me, she said, 'And now we have Mr Thompson who is going to speak about Folk Lore in the Dales.'

I was not Mr Thompson and my subject was not folk lore but rather than embarrass her in front of her audience (or perhaps because I felt she should be taught a gentle lesson), I spoke about folk lore from the dales, a subject with which I was familiar and for which I required no lecture notes. At the conclusion I answered a few questions in the guise of Mr Thompson (whoever he was) and received a vote of thanks which went, 'Please show your appreciate to Mr Thompson for his excellent talk about our local folk lore'. And so I went home wondering what would happen when the real Mr Thompson turned up, probably the following month.

Apart from speaking to a variety of local groups perhaps one of the oddest tasks I was asked to do was to look after a baby in its pram while the mother popped out to the shop. I was on a routine foot patrol of Aidensfield one morning when young Mrs Jenny Warren suddenly opened her front door just as I was strolling past in my uniform. She was a bouncy young woman with a mop of fair hair, an infectious smile and a very attractive personality. Everyone liked Jenny.

'Ah, Mr Rhea, glad I caught you, I saw you walking past.'

''Morning Jenny, can I help?'

'I hope you don't mind my asking, but when I saw you through the window, I thought I couldn't miss the opportunity.'

'Go on,' I invited with some curiosity.

'Can you look after Jeremy for a few minutes?'

'Jeremy?'

'My baby, he's fast asleep in his pram, and I have to get something urgently from the shop. I'll only be a couple of minutes. He is asleep but if I move the pram he will wake up and need changing, but if he does wake up his bottle is on the oven top . . .'

'Well, I'm not sure . . .'

'Two minutes, that's all. Just to pop into the shop.'

'Can I get whatever you want from the shop? I'm going that way.' I thought that suggestion was a good compromise.

'I don't think so,' and she blushed slightly. 'It's women's things, if you understand, you being a married man . . . and it wouldn't be nice for you carrying packets of such things through the street in uniform so I thought . . .'

'Oh, I see. All right then. Two minutes.'

Taking off my cap, I went inside where she showed me the sleeping child in his pram and then his bottle on top of the oven; it was warm, I noticed.

'I prepared it a few minutes ago, ready for when he wakes up,' she oozed. 'It'll be fine, not too hot . . . so if he wakes up, which he won't, just give it to him as you would at home with your own.'

And then she rushed out. I saw her racing past the window as I sat down in an armchair beside the pram. I was pleased to see the child was fast asleep. I knew the family and this was their first and only child. Jenny's husband, Alan, worked as a mechanic in Ashfordly in one of the garages and they were a nice couple. I found myself somewhat flattered at being trusted to undertake this responsibility.

After all, two minutes wasn't a very long time. The two minutes ticked by. Then another two. And another two . . . six minutes became ten, and then fifteen. I got up and went to the door, opening it to look up and down the street, and I felt rather furtive. What would the neighbours think of the bobby peering suspiciously out of an attractive young woman's house while her husband was at work? But there was no sign of Jenny.

Then Jeremy woke up.

I heard him begin to stir in his pram and at first there were gurgles and chuckles but they soon became a whimper and then a bawling kind of yell that could surely be heard halfway to Ashfordly. That'll fetch Mum, I thought. But it didn't. I had to lift him out and from the aroma that surrounded him I knew he needed a nappy change but I was not about to do that. Besides, I had not been instructed in the skills of nappy changing in this small household and so I gently lifted him from the pram, placed him in the crook of my arm and went into the kitchen to get his bottle. During those few minutes he stopped crying but then, as we neared the kitchen, he took a long hard look at me and began to thrash his arms and bawl his head off.

I grabbed his bottle and hurried back to the lounge where I re-settled in the armchair and, using all the skills I had learned when my own brood was little, tried to feed him. But he was having none of it. He kept staring at me with his eyes wide open as he yelled and yelled as if all the hounds in hell were chasing him. And then I realized I was still wearing my peaked cap. Perhaps that had frightened him? I removed it. Then I heard the front door open—thank goodness Jenny had returned. But it wasn't her. It was her mother who lived in Elsinby, Mrs Corner. I knew her and she knew me. Thank goodness we weren't strangers.

'Oh, my gracious!' cried Mrs Corner. 'Has something happened? Where's Jenny? And what are you doing to Jeremy?'

And without waiting for an explanation she zoomed in and lifted the child from my arms to cradle him in hers while making cooing noises. She reminded me of a wood pigeon on its nest. That seemed to pacify the child because he looked at her and stopped his awful noise, gurgling up at his granny as if the bottle and its contents did not matter.

'So what's happened, Mr Rhea?' asked Granny Corner when things had calmed down a little. She moved across to the other armchair and settled down with the now peaceful child in her arms, sucking at the bottle I had passed to her.

'I was walking past when Jenny rushed out to ask if I would look after Jeremy for a couple of minutes while she went to the shop,' I explained. 'That was twenty minutes ago. She's not been back. She'd left that bottle for him but I think he's frightened of policemen. He will be now, surely, waking up to find a bobby staring down at him. I took my cap off, I think that calmed him down a bit.'

'Well, Jenny would know I was due to call in about now, I usually do at this time of day.'

'She must have met someone and got chatting. Anyway, Jeremy's in good hands, thanks to you.'

'You've been very kind Mr Rhea,' she smiled. 'But don't let me delay you. And thanks. I am sure Jenny has a perfectly sensible explanation for asking you to do such a thing.'

And so I prepared to leave, putting my cap back on my head. This prompted Jeremy to start bawling all over again and so I took my leave, bidding farewell to Mrs Corner but deciding not to terrify the child any more than necessary.

As I crept out, however, Jenny was hurrying towards me. An expression of concern flitted across her face as she saw me leaving the house.

'I'm not abandoning him, your mum's arrived,' I explained.

'Sorry about that, Mr Rhea, but old Mrs Penshaw two doors down called me in, she couldn't get her fire going. I went into help but the grate was full of ash and I had to clean it out, then there was no coal so I had to borrow some from next door and then her paper and sticks were damp . . . I couldn't leave her.'

'Well done,' I said. 'It was a pleasure.'

'I did get her fire going but hope I haven't held you up,' she produced one of her winning smiles and I capitulated.

'Not in the slightest,' but I must admit I worried in case little Jeremy grew up to fear men in peaked caps. Having experienced what he thought of police officers in their peaked caps I wondered what he would make of the postman. Or engine drivers.

It would be impossible to describe all the non-police events and activities I attended in my efforts to help others during my few years in Aidensfield but I remember once clambering into a woman's loft to rescue or release a sparrow that had become trapped inside. Covered in dust and dirt, I managed to persuade it to leave via the loft window which I could open a fraction but had no idea how it had got in there.

Then there was Mrs Crawshaw's cat that had got its head stuck in a metal drainpipe. I had to take cat and a section of the pipe to a local garage to persuade the owner to cut open the section of pipe without being scratched by the terrified cat. And he did so. There was also the time I found myself taking eight children to playschool in the police mini-van because their regular transport had broken down. Happily, Sergeant Blaketon was on his day off at that time and did not catch me.

If he had caught me doing that, I don't think he would have taken any official action against me, except to mutter something about the misuse of official vehicles.

Perhaps the most vulnerable of people on my beat were the elderly. Fortunately there were plenty of people in the village who would ensure such individuals were not abandoned; they included the postman, shopkeeper, Catholic priest, vicar, neighbours and those without any specific role and of course I would keep an eye open in case anyone needed help but was afraid to ask. There were always indications that help might be required—matters like no smoke rising from their chimneys, no lights inside the house when it was dark, full milk bottles collecting on the doorstep, curtains remaining closed or post gathering in the letter box. There were many other indications that someone required help and most of us recognized those, and reacted accordingly.

That kind of attention is commonplace in a village community while in a town or city it can be construed as prying or being too inquisitive but within a small village the residents are rather like an extended family. They care for one another and do not resent others genuinely seeking or offering assistance and advice. Many are only too glad to know they can rely on receiving that type of well-meant attention.

I can recall helping one old lady who had constant trouble lighting her living room fire simply because she never cleaned the ash from the grate; I would pop in every few days to clean it out for her. Another aged about eighty-four used to wander up the village street in the coldest of weather clad in nothing more than a thin blouse and equally thin skirt. Whenever I stopped her she would tell me she was going to visit her mother and so I would say that her mum had gone out and so I would take her home—until next time.

Perhaps the most resilient of the elderly population of Aidensfield was 87-years-old Stanley Marshall, a retired businessman who had previously opened popular department stores in York, Leeds, Beverley and Scarborough. Quite unexpectedly, I found myself involved with him in a most interesting way and I suppose that brief relationship was an example of the type of service available in a village community. It happened like this.

Mr Marshall was much wealthier than most of the villagers and despite his age, was surprisingly active and alert. A widower, he had two sons and two daughters, all now approaching their sixtieth year; he also had grandchildren and great grandchildren. All his own children had earlier worked for, and now ran, the family business although he remained chairman, and they lived variously in York, Leeds, Beverley and Scarborough, each running their local Marshall's store. They were very successful in managing those branches which, as always, generated an income for Stanley. He was proud that some of his grandchildren were now closely involved and so the family links would continue. Since the death of his wife, Alice, he had looked after himself albeit with a daily help, Mrs Sinclair, who cleaned and cooked for him while ensuring that he was well-cared for.

His stone-built house was one of the largest in Aidensfield, slightly smaller than Aidensfield Hall but large enough to be considered one of the most impressive and desirable in the district. Situated on an elevated site at the end of a drive that was at least a mile and a half in length, it was known as Aidensfield Grange. The turning and twisting drive with some surprisingly steep inclines passed through a copse of mature woodland that he also owned. His long drive skirted the river, literally running along the bank in places, until it terminated in front of the house.

The Grange was surrounded by several acres of fertile land along with a beautiful garden, large lawn, two tennis courts, a croquet pitch and that patch of mature woodland. Although modest by the standards of some other nearby estates, his still required the full-time attention of a gardener and woodman but it was that part of his land closest to the house that Mr Stanley enjoyed most in his leisure hours. He loved his garden and his privacy but would allow the villagers into his grounds, either just to wander around to admire the plants on certain days or perhaps to hold a fund-raising fete of some kind. He had no objection to them entering his distant woodland to seek fallen timber for firewood, logs or kindling, or to walk their dogs or simply to stroll among the trees but he did not want them to light any fires.

His daily help, Mrs Sinclair, did not live in his house. She came from the village, a widow, who enjoyed his companionship along with the modest wage he paid her. Either she would cycle to her work at his house or sometimes he would collect her in his car, especially if the weather was inclement. Although she regarded him as a friend, he managed to maintain that master-servant relationship, doubtless through his experience in dealing with the staff of his commercial empire. Even without Mrs Sinclair's help he was always very well dressed, usually in differing shades of green or brown, and might even have been considered dapper.

He always had an immaculate haircut, neat moustache, clean shoes and smart clothes. Everyone in Aidensfield knew him as Mr Stanley and when he walked along the street, he was always greeted with a smile and chat which he returned with evident pleasure. Apart from describing his house and garden as his pride and joy, and occasionally using the term for all his offspring or indeed referring to his clutch of stores in that way, his real pride and joy was his Jaguar car. It was a 1957 XK 140 in pastel blue with a grey interior, a two-seater sports car with an open top.

It was always in pristine condition and he loved cruising around the countryside on fine days with the hood down and the wind blowing through his hair—and he had a good head of pure white hair, beautifully trimmed. He had bought his Jaguar when it was new but somehow managed to keep it clean even after driving on muddy rural roads and along his equally muddy lane. How he achieved that was always a mystery—but he kept his shoes very clean too. He was that sort of man. Crisp and clean.

It was very rarely that I had cause to visit him at home, such occasions perhaps being the renewal of his firearm certificate or to warn him of travelling criminals who were targeting large, isolated houses. He did not keep livestock or run a farm so I had no stock registers to check but he always made my visits a pleasure and was keen to learn about the responsibilities and work of modern police forces.

He would often joke that he had never passed a driving test because he had started his driving career long before tests were introduced in 1935. He would entertain me with tales of driving on empty roads without speed limits and before the appearance of hazards like roundabouts and pedestrian crossings with automatic signals. He told me that pedestrian crossings controlled by traffic lights had been installed in London before the turn of the 20th century. The lights permitted pedestrians to cross in safety but in fact they held up the traffic for far too long.

No one could build lights that changed more quickly and so those early crossings were abandoned although they were reintroduced some years later when the lights problem had been solved. During our wide-ranging chats, Mrs Sinclair always offered a cup of tea or coffee, and a biscuit of some kind. Those occasions were very pleasant indeed.

Then a catastrophe happened.

My phone rang one Saturday morning in April when I was off duty and seriously considering some work in the garden, perhaps beginning my efforts by cutting the lawn. The caller was Mrs Sinclair.

'Can you come quickly, Mr Rhea, Mr Stanley has had a nasty accident.'

I was tempted to say I was off duty and would arrange for another officer to attend, but this involved Mr Stanley whom I considered a friend. I decided to attend but first needed to know more about it should it be necessary to alert the various emergency agencies such as doctor, hospital, ambulance or breakdown services.

'What's happened?'

'He's run off the road in his car, down near the river, he's all right but soaking wet and his car is upside down in the water . . .'

'He's all right, you say?'

'Yes, shaken a little and very wet, but he's not hurt. He walked home.'

'So where is his car?'

'In the river beside his drive, that narrow bit where there is a slight bend but he ran off the road and somehow got into the river, the car's upside down in that shallow stretch . . . he got thrown out so he's very lucky, he could have drowned.'

'Anyone else involved? Any other vehicle? Horse? Car, bike, cart? Pedestrian?'

'No, just him, nothing else.'

Then I realized the accident had occurred on private land with only the owner of the property and his car involved. That meant it was not the official concern of the police and would not be recorded as a road traffic accident, so it had to be dealt with in a different manner, but not by me. It was the responsibility of his insurers.

'I'll come straight away,' I promised even though I was not obliged to attend. 'So where is Mr Stanley now?'

'He's not hurt so I sent him upstairs to get all his wet clothes off and have a bath, then put on some dry things. He's up there now, I expect he'll be another quarter of an hour.'

'That gives me time to have a look at the scene and decide what needs to be done. I'll be there shortly. Do you think he needs a doctor to examine him? He's no spring chicken, as they say, I hope he hasn't done himself an injury.'

'He wouldn't have a doctor in the house, Mr Rhea, so don't do that. He's quite all right with no sign of an injury although he might have a few bruises. Nothing else, no broken bones, no sign of blood or cuts. I expect there'll be aches and pains tomorrow though.'

'Thanks for all that, you can tell him I'm on my way.'

As I drove my private car along the riverside track to Aidensfield Grange, I could see the lovely blue Jaguar upside down in the water. Parts of it were submerged but the wheels, engine compartment and boot were protruding above the surface and it looked rather like a large dead cat sitting in a puddle. The river was quite shallow here and there were submerged rocks too. The car seemed to be resting on some of them and that had kept most of its bodywork and mechanical bits out of the water, but by any standards, it was a sad sight.

I could see where it had veered off the track because there were tyre marks on the verge and I noticed a large stone protruding from the road surface on the side nearest the river. I wondered if he had hit that with a front wheel and lost control. A heavy bump like that could easily jerk the steering wheel from the driver's hand, especially if he was aged.

There was no other obstruction on the road, although it was unsurfaced and rather rough in places. Clearly he'd shot off the road, perhaps at speed, and the car had overturned—then I noticed a short but sturdy tree stump protruding from the river bank. It bore signs of very recent damage. I reckoned his car had swerved off the road, hit that stump and somersaulted into the water. It must have been very spectacular. Amazingly he'd been thrown clear of the open-top car to land in the water which was only about two feet deep at this point. I felt relieved he had not been in a conventional car with a roof—that might have trapped him especially as such a roof might have collapsed in the crash. Fortunately he'd not been rendered unconscious and had obviously been able to walk out of the river. With no one else and no other vehicle involved, it looked like an unfortunate accident but because it had not occurred on a public road, I would not need to submit any kind of official report. Likewise there would be no question of considering careless driving or any associated traffic offence. I would, however, make a record for my own files.

I was relieved and pleased that Mr Stanley was not injured although I reckoned his car would need some careful attention—I could not see what damage lurked under the water but it might not be too bad. The car's engine and most of its operational parts were not submerged.

When I arrived at the house Mrs Sinclair led me into the lounge where Mr Stanley was sitting in a winged chair clutching a huge tumbler of whisky but otherwise looking as immaculate as ever in his smart dry clothing.

'How about sharing a tot with me, Mr Rhea, I see you are not on duty.'

'Just a very little thank you, I have to drive home remember, although most of the trip will be on private roads.'

'Shall I make some coffee?' asked Mrs Sinclair.

'A good idea, Mrs Sinclair, yes,' said the master of the house as he poured me a generous dash of fine malt whisky. If it became necessary I could always leave my car here and walk home.

When we were settled and while Mrs Sinclair attended to her duties in the kitchen, I asked, 'So what happened, Mr Stanley?'

'I've no idea, Mr Rhea. There I was tootling along the track on my way home from the village minding my own business and suddenly I hit something pretty damned solid and the next thing I knew I was flying through the air to land in the river with my car upside down beside me. Fortunately not on top of me! I'm not hurt but a little surprised but I do fear for my lovely car. I am sorry to have caused you to come out when you are not on duty.'

'I wanted to check that you were not injured or that there were no other problems, Mr Stanley. But this is not a police matter, it is not on a public road and in any case no one else is involved. It is purely a matter for you and your insurers.'

'Really? Well, I find that very reassuring, I do hate all the formalities that go with official matters, there's always so much paperwork and filling-in of endless forms. So what can I do about my car?'

'If I were you, I'd first ring your insurance agent or the insurance company. They will have procedures for dealing with such matters, even when they occur on private property.'

'Ah, that is no problem, they know me well.'

'Good, but however, they might not want the car removed or touched until their assessors have examined it. And they might allow you to hire a car until a decision is reached about your vehicle and its roadworthiness. That's all you can do—but I must ask whether you require a doctor? You might have taken a hidden knock.'

'Not at all, Mr Rhea, I am absolutely fine with no cuts and bruises and no broken bones. The water softened my flight when I landed in it. And this glass of malt will cope with any effects of shock I might be suffering. If it doesn't, I'll have another. Or perhaps two.'

After spending some forty minutes with him as he reminisced about his past exploits and laughed off the current dilemma, I made sure he could cope with everything that had to be done, and left him as Mrs Sinclair took away the cups and glasses. She escorted me to the door and assured me that Mr Stanley was quite all right—she would remain with him for the rest of the day and would inform his family of the incident. It would go into my official note book as an incident not an accident and so, as far as I was concerned, the matter was closed. Marvelling that the old man could have survived this event with so few signs of distress or injury, I could return to my lawn mowing and enjoy the rest of my weekend off.

It would be five or six days later that I received a telephone call one evening when I was off duty. A male voice said, 'Hello, Mr Rhea. My name is Alan Marshall, Stanley's eldest son. I live in Leeds. We haven't met, but he has often talked about you.'

'Ah, hello Mr Marshall. And how is your father?'

'As fit as ever, you'd never think he was nearly drowned or that his precious car is recovering from damp and distress. Thanks for the advice you gave him—he got in touch with his insurance company as you suggested and you'll be pleased to know that they will cover the cost of recovering the car from the river, and any repairs it needs. It doesn't need much, fortunately; the water was quite shallow and the car was resting on submerged rocks. There are a few dents and scratches but it should be back on the road in a couple of months or so.'

'Thanks for telling me, I appreciate it.'

'Actually there is another reason for calling—the insurance company is not very happy about continuing Dad's car insurance. The accident has drawn attention to his age and they are questioning his fitness to drive. The problem is twofold—the first clearly is his age but the second is that no one is quite sure how his car managed to get into the river upside down. Not even Dad can explain that, he reckons he was not driving very fast, but the surface of that drive is not the best by any means. It's all bumps and holes, more like an ancient Roman road than an English driveway.'

'I agree. I think he hit a hidden rock that was protruding from the surface of his drive, Mr Marshall, the sudden jerk could have loosened his grip of the steering wheel and diverted the front wheels to make the car veer sharply to its left and collide with a short but thick tree stump. A nearby stump has been damaged which supports that theory and I think that caused the Jaguar to flip over as it did. Luckily your dad was thrown out and landed in shallow water. I think we'd need a stunt man to replicate that incident!'

'I agree with your assessment and think it was a one-off incident, Mr Rhea, a chance in a million.'

'I'd go along with that. After all, he has been driving for years and years without incident, and he must have known his own drive very well.'

'For those and all sorts of other reasons, I think my dad should not have his insurance cover taken from him. He's never had any other accident in all his years of driving. We, the family that is, intend to challenge the insurance company's conclusions.'

'How can you do that?'

'They're demanding a driving test drive for Dad, and a medical examination. For the driving test he would be put through all the situations that would face a person taking a standard test, including his eyesight but especially the speed of his reactions.'

'And if he fails, he will be grounded?'

'That's what it amounts to, yes.'

'I can't say I'm surprised even though this happened on private land,' I admitted. 'I'm sure he will sail through all his tests, so how does this involve me?'

'Dad will not agree to undergo a driving test without some advance preparation. He's never had an accident in his entire life until now and his eyesight is perfect with his reactions being as fast as anyone else's . . .'

'I realize that, but he must now prove those points to his insurance company—that is quite standard procedure after incidents of the kind he was involved in. No one is trying to take him off the road, they just want him to prove he is still capable despite his age. By taking the test, he will convince the county council that he is fit to retain his driving licence. They could rescind it if the insurer's demand that; the fact he never took a test in the first place is not relevant here. In fact, he's got everything to gain from this—and a few more years on the road, hopefully.'

'He's got everything to gain except his pride, Mr Rhea.'

'Oh dear! So what are you suggesting?'

'He wants you to assess him.'

'Me? But I am not a qualified driving examiner or tutor.'

'But you've passed the police tests? You must have done so because you drive an official police vehicle as part of your duty.'

'Yes, I've been on a police driving course as well as taking the ordinary civilian driving test.'

'Exactly. He values your experience and would like you to take him out in his car when it's back on the road. He wants you to find and correct any faults he might have whether it's slow reactions or lack of knowledge about the Highway Code or the need for more skill in coping with modern traffic conditions. To coach him in other words. He doesn't care if it takes six months or a year, but once you are sure he is up to scratch, he will take any test his insurers or the licensing authority ask of him. And even a medical test. So my question is—will you do it?'

I had to think hard and fast before replying, after a brief pause I said, 'I will help all I can, but I do not want payment of any kind, I am doing this as a friend. I must stress though that I am not a qualified driving instructor and cannot guarantee to train him to the standard required to pass a formal test. I can only throw a few tasks in his way!'

'He does understand that, Mr Rhea. Dad is a very astute and wise man.'

'All right, tell him I will help all I can. Ask him to call me when he's ready and I'll do my best to accommodate him.'

'He does insist on using his own car.'

'I can understand that, it's the one he's familiar with.'

And so the deal was done.

Mr Stanley's lovely old Jaguar was back on the road within six weeks, with all its dents removed and all signs of its partial immersion in the river no longer visible. The engine ran as smoothly as ever and everything else worked as new. In that lovely old car, therefore, I undertook several outings with Stanley depending upon which shift I was working. I took him out at night and in the daytime, I took him onto the old airfield used by police drivers as a skid-pan, and I made him drive though York, Leeds and Scarborough, all very busy places especially at weekends.

He coped surprisingly well with hill starts, traffic lights, one-way streets, roundabouts, pedestrian crossings, narrow parking spaces, wet and muddy roads, sudden and emergency stops, technical matters like brakes, gears, lights and oil pressure, questions about the Highway Code and even modest matters of motoring law. He executed three-point turns, reversed into confined spaces, coped with school-children, dogs, sheep and cattle and even a few water-slashes or fords as some were known. Try though I did, I could not seriously fault him. He did falter once or twice in some of the manoeuvres and tests I laid on for him but quickly recognized and corrected any problems. After several weeks of tough tests that I had produced for him, we did not have hard words or fall out with each other. He was the ideal pupil, still keen to learn in spite of his age. I had to agree that he was fit to take any official driving test and he said he would respond accordingly to his insurers. Before their test was arranged, he passed the required medical and eyesight tests.

On a fine day some months after his accident, I accompanied him to the testing station and left him to face his ordeal. When he returned he was beaming—the examiner had pronounced him fit to drive. With me at his side, off he went in his splendid old Jaguar and on the way, he stopped at an off-licence to buy me a bottle of champagne.

'Have a drink on me,' he was so pleased with himself. 'And next time you come to The Grange you must bring your wife and we'll have a proper celebration.'

'I'd love that.'

He dropped me off at my police house and offered me a fee for my tuition, but I had to decline on the grounds it was contrary to police regulations. The champagne was most acceptable and he warned me to expect a Christmas present later in the year, probably in the shape of a fine case of malt whisky.

I did not decline that either—my help had not been part of my police duty.

But on his way home through the trees that lined his drive, something happened and instead of somersaulting into the river he collided head-on with a massive oak. He was not hurt, but his precious car received a broken offside headlight, a crumpled offside mudguard and a buckled bumper bar.

I never asked what had occurred even though Mrs Sinclair thought I should (most discreetly) be aware of the incident. He paid for the repairs without involving his insurance company.

Officially, however, I never knew about it and like his earlier mishap, it was of no concern to the police as it had occurred on private property. Neither Stanley's family nor his insurance company were made aware of that second incident and so he continued to drive without further problems along the highways and byways around rural Yorkshire.

He was still driving aged 99, some years after I had left Aidensfield.

CHAPTER 7

During my years at Aidensfield, I had witnessed the change from bicycle as a means of transport for rural bobbies to radio-equipped mini-vans along with massive developments in the scientific investigation of crime. Specialised computers were currently undergoing tests while personal radio sets were being assessed for possible operational use. It was these developments along with the ever-present pressure to spend less money that meant I had to leave my police house in its spectacular hilltop setting at Aidensfield; I was part of those changes.

Much of my final work involved the notification of individuals and businesses of my impending departure along with advice on how and where to contact the police after I had left. With my faithful typewriter and a photocopier, I printed leaflets to leave at strategic places so that the information was readily available. One part of my duties—the inspection of livestock registers on farms—was to be taken over by the Ministry of Agriculture Fisheries and Food and this development did not appeal to many farmers. As one of them said, 'I don't want strangers in suits wandering all over my land—when t'bobby comes in uniform I know who he is.' Before leaving, however, I would ensure that all the livestock registers on my beat had been checked.

Perhaps the greatest challenge was to claim that every reported crime had been thoroughly investigated and that the perpetrator(s) had been identified and dealt with. But a 100% clear-up rate was impossible. Many minor crimes would never be detected, quite often because they were committed by criminals who might be miles away before their actions were discovered and many did not leave a trace of evidence.

Happily, however, the crime rate on Aidensfield beat (which included eight other small villages) had always been very low and I was satisfied I had done all that was possible to detect any outstanding crimes, however minor they might be.

I was confident I would not be leaving any *major* crimes undetected—with one exception. On my beat there was one very mysterious murder that had never been solved and whose perpetrator had never been identified or brought to justice. It was locally known as the Murkmire Murder or sometimes the Murkmire Mystery, but I doubt if anyone living outside a rather small area of bleak moorland around Aidensfield had ever heard of it. Certainly the case had never appeared in any collected accounts of unsolved murders, local or otherwise, and there were times when I wondered if it was nothing more than a legend or myth because so little was known about it. In spite of that uncertainty, the name of the crime continued to be repeated by local people, almost as if it had happened very recently or within the collective memory of their ancestors. It had become part of local folklore.

Even I, as a comparative newcomer to Aidensfield, knew that local parents warned their children not to venture over Murkmire in the darkness in case something nasty happened to them. The tale was one of those yarns that are passed down the generations without anyone determining its origins or truthfulness and to my knowledge, no one—not even I—had delved into its history. It remained a mystery.

The uninhabited moorland around Murkmire was higher than the surrounding landscape, rising to around 1,000 feet (305 metres) above sea level. It was a bleak and rocky place with gorse bushes growing among tufts of bracken and heather on the slopes. Ten miles or so to the east was the North Sea and the fishing village of Robin Hood's Bay, once a notorious haunt of smugglers and that area of sea is visible from Murkmire tops.

Although this mire-laden area looks flat from a distance, several parts of it contain saucer-shaped depressions. These are quite close to the summit but, because over the past centuries any rainwater or snow-melt could not flow away from them, they developed into bogs, marshland or even small ponds or tarns.

Those boggy parts are known as mires in this part of Yorkshire. Wise travellers never ventured across a stretch of mire even when solid tufts of reeds or peat seemed to provide stepping-stones through the mess; a slip could be fatal because some of the bogs had the effect of quicksand and in a matter of seconds could swallow an entire human body or an unwary animal like a stray sheep.

There were plenty of other footpaths across the moors, most having been in use for centuries and some were paved with well-worn sandstone slabs. These were often called trods or monks' trods because, in times past, they would link the many abbeys and priories that were a feature of this remote moorland and the dales below. The trods had long been used by pedestrians and horses, sometimes with trains of pack-horses trekking across those bleak heights with their precious loads in the most appalling of weather. There is no doubt some routes were used by smugglers as they distributed their contraband from ship to customer. Evidence of those trods exists to this day and in some cases those centuries-old stones remain in position and are still used by determined hikers. Sadly, many of the trods closer to centres of population were destroyed in the last century during road-widening schemes, and their sandstone slabs broken up. Even without the stone slabs, however, many of those old tracks remain as green routes and are popularly used as footpaths by hikers, people riding mountain bikes or even those with motor bikes or off-road vehicles.

Despite the popularity and spectacular setting of that stretch of moorland, few of its modern explorers or visitors are aware of the Murkmire Murder.

It is occasionally mentioned in tourist literature or local history books, but always as a legend with no suggestion that it could be true. There was a distinct lack of supportive facts about it. The sum of our knowledge, scant though it was, came from folk memories that have been handed down the generations.

The tale is on a par with the barguest of Egton and the gytrash of Goathland, terrible in the past but now forgotten. Thus history, legend, folk lore and modern storytelling became intermingled and serve to conceal the basic facts. The true story, if one ever existed, has been lost in the mists of time. So was there really a murder here in ancient times? It's rather like Robin Hood—no one knows for sure whether the outlaw and his merry men actually existed or whether he is a myth based on the activities of the Knights Templar but stories, films and television dramas continue to feature his exploits, albeit much altered. Similarly, St George, famous for killing dragons and rescuing maidens in distress is also a legendary figure with no known facts about his life, even if he is the patron saint of England. These examples show that a good legend can eventually become accepted as the truth, especially when its origins date to a time when few stories and fewer facts were committed to paper. Many of our surviving legends were the work of itinerant story-tellers or minstrels who told and re-told the stories without setting them down in writing. And the people continued—and still continue—to tell them with improvements, alterations and additions.

During my tenure at Aidensfield I had heard several references to this mystery but nothing specific such as dates, the method of death nor the name of the victim. The only hint of truth, and perhaps the only fact, was that it had occurred on that patch of dangerous moorland still known as Murkmire. It was when news of my impending departure began to circulate among the community that one old character called Ben Tomkins reminded me of it.

He was sitting in the Brewers' Arms with four or five or his mates, enjoying a lunchtime pint or two when I called.

'Thoo's done a grand job for us, Mr Rhea, but thoo's still not arrested that chap for t'Murkmire Murder.'

'That was centuries ago, Ben, long before I was posted here,' I gave a bland answer because I then knew so little about the case.

'Was it? So do you know when it happened?' he asked cheekily.

'I've no idea,' I admitted. 'I've not done any research into the case but from what I have been told, it was a long, long time ago, centuries even.'

'Aye, centuries ago they reckon,' smiled Ben. 'But most of them constables who've served in Aidensfield before you came 'ave tried to solve it, or even tried to put a name to t'chap who died.'

'Have they? And did they get a result?'

'Not them, Mr Rhea, nobody's any wiser. There's nowt much about it in books. All we know is that summat nasty 'appened up on Murkmire and they say a fellow got away with murder. And we still don't know who the dead chap was. He can't have been local fellow can he, if t'villagers didn't know who he was?'

'That's a good point, but who are 'They'? Who says a man got away with murder?' I asked.

'Well, folks hereabouts, them that tells t'tale, they all say that. That's how t'tale's been told for years in these parts. Passed down from family to family, generation to generation. Not that it would be any good finding out who did it, he'll be dead and gone. You couldn't arrest him even if you did find his name.'

'So it might not be true?' I put to him. 'It might be nothing but a story, some tale that's been made up, something that's survived from the Dark Ages? Long before history was written down?'

I could sense from his reactions and those of his pals that they did not like the suggestion the story was not true or perhaps they could not appreciate how ancient the history of those moors could be—people had lived here since the Stone Age. Clearly, with all those characters being locally born and bred, they had been brought up with that tale in their background and it had become regarded as part of Aidensfield's real history. It was a prevailing mystery that would never be solved and it would have been told, re-told and greatly embroidered around many firesides on dark evenings when storytelling and ghost tales were commonplace. In considering the tale, I had to admit it was a real mystery yet I had never tried to establish its truth. Perhaps I should?

'Well, Mr Rhea, some of us thought you might have found out a bit more about it, seeing you write about such things.'

'I wish I'd had this conversation with you when I first arrived, I could have spent some time delving into the case, but I'll tell you what, Ben. I'll start now, even though I might not finish my enquiries before I leave. And if I find out anything, I'll come back and tell you. And buy you all a pint. How's that?'

'Aye, well, it would be nice to know a bit more about it. Even if it's nowt but a story, it must have started somewhere.'

'That's a very good point, Ben. So leave it with me.'

'There'll be a pint or two waiting for you an' all if you do find summat out and tell us who did it,' he promised and I assured him I would return. But with so many things to finalize before I left, especially when trying to buy a house in this locality, I had more than enough to occupy me.

In thinking about it, though, the story did present a challenge and I found myself increasingly determined to ferret out the truth and I would continue even after leaving Aidensfield. As Ben had said, the yarn must have started somewhere.

It was perhaps fortunate that one of my removal chores lent itself to some modest if hurried research. I owned lots of books many of which formed a good collection of local history, and I also had others containing local legends, folk lore, customs, dialect and associated topics. All those would have to be packed ready for removal and it was in the midst of doing so that I could quickly check through their indices to see whether any referred to the supposed murder or even specifically to the location known as Murkmire. And so I warmed to my self-imposed task as I began to wonder whether I would or could solve this outstanding murder before I left Aidensfield. It seemed highly unlikely because if others had tried and failed, did I stand any chance of success? Despite the lack of time, I would give it my best efforts.

Over the course of several days as I carefully packed and arranged my library of books in subject order, the information I gleaned was very slight indeed. I found just one reference to the Murkmire Murder. In a small but old volume of essays about Aidensfield—'*Some Reminiscences of Aidensfield and District*' by Aaron Harland which he had published privately in 1876—I found a sentence that read, 'It is said by the older people of this parish that years ago a terrible murder was committed near Murkmire, but that the felon was never apprehended.' And that was all. No name for the killer or victim and no date of the supposed crime. But it was a start.

I decided to compile a Murkmire Murder notebook full of such references with their sources because, after even a short time, it is difficult to recall the whereabouts of some very important snippets of information unless they are catalogued. The snag with that particular gem was that it contained nothing factual.

It was hearsay and proved absolutely nothing except that the supposed crime had been discussed and remembered around a century earlier but it did mean I had an approximate starting date. Clearly Mr Harland, the author, had thought the case was real but it was evident he had not researched it. Perhaps he had tried, without success?

At that stage, my police trained instincts began to churn around in my head as I was patrolling in my mini-van or performing quiet foot patrols in tranquil areas. Momentarily it took my mind off Greengrass, pumas and house-hunting and I realized that if the murder had actually happened, even as long ago as medieval times, there would have been an inquest and a burial. The coroner of the day should have been informed and he would have come to inspect the body because that was his duty. That had been part of our history and investigative procedures for centuries and as such, there should be a record of this case.

The office of coroner dates into the mists of English history with its origins probably in 1194 although the first coroners' duties were mainly clerical. Later a famous statute—*De Officio Coronatoris*—was passed in 1276 and it commanded:

A coroner shall go to the place where any person is slain or suddenly dead or wounded . . . and he should summon a jury out of four or five neighbouring towns to make enquiry upon view of the body, and the coroner and jury should enquire into the manner of the killing.

Although that statute has since been repealed, it established the role of the coroner and it remains his duty to view the body and to arrange a post-mortem if the cause of death is not known or suspected not to be by natural causes. The system, with all its variations, operated throughout the Middle Ages but a threat to coroners arose in the fourteenth century when the newly created magistrates began to conduct preliminary investigations into persons suspected of homicide.

The magistrates gained control over coroners' official functions and from the end of the fifteenth century until 1751, the office of coroner ceased to be of any real importance in the judicial system. In 1751, however, an Act of Parliament was passed that virtually revived the office and duties of the coroner, and by the nineteenth century their powers had again been strengthened. So had those changes affected this murder and its investigation? Could there be gaps in the records of local inquests between the fifteenth century and the seventeenth?

These developments meant that the date of the Murkmire Murder was crucial—if it had occurred between the fifteenth and even the eighteenth centuries there may not have been an inquest by a specific coroner, simply a case presided over by a magistrate. I became determined to find out. Luckily, a former colleague had recently retired from the Force to secure a post in the County Record Office—and if any records of such an inquest existed, they would surely be somewhere in the files of that establishment. So I rang him. His name was Bernard.

'Good morning, Bernard, it's Nick Rhea speaking from Aidensfield. How's the new job going?'

He enthused about it, saying his task was to sort through all the miscellaneous documents that arrived in the Record Office and to make sure they were stored in the right places and carefully indexed then cross-referenced. Experts were on hand to translate them and some very old papers required special preservative treatment. He added there was no pressure to complete things immediately as so often happened in the police service—the police were accustomed to responding promptly to events and incidents, but not these record keepers. They must not and could not rush their work—it was far too important.

He soon guessed I had a favour to ask.

'So, Nick, have you got something to donate to the Record Office or are you after something from us?'

'I need some information from your files,' and so I explained about the Murkmire Murder while referring to Aaron Harland's reference in his book. I concluded by saying, 'I wonder whether there was an inquest or whether your office contains any old files of relevance. If so, you might advise me how to locate them.'

'It's the sort of thing we might have here,' he agreed. 'So is Murkmire very close to Aidensfield? In Aidensfield Parish for example?'

'Yes, on the moors just outside the village, certainly within Aidensfield Parish. In the past, I think it would have been within Ashfordly Petty Sessional Division too, the town used to have its own Quarter Sessions and magistrates' court so if there are any records, they should be retained somewhere.'

'So precisely what do you want to know?'

'I want to know if the murder actually occurred and if so when. It would be nice to get the name of the victim or even where he was buried, and of course, whether anyone was prosecuted for the crime, along with the name of the killer. It's quite a tall order and I wondered if you could help by pointing me in the right direction. I am prepared to come along to the Record Office if necessary but not for a while because I'm packing ready to be transferred to our training department.'

'Well done! That's right up your street,' he said. 'Now if the records are lodged here they should contain all that sort of stuff. Leave it with me, Nick, I'll do what I can for you, it'll make a nice change from simply filing stuff and recording facts, or getting old records translated into modern English. A lot of them are in Latin. Anyway, you can always come to make your own searches although it's wise to telephone in advance, especially if you need help.'

'Once I get settled into my new post at Solberge, I may do that and I might even take you out for lunch and a couple of pints.'

'Now you're talking!' he laughed. 'But meanwhile, leave it with me. It might take me a few days or even weeks. Sometimes we strike lucky and at others we have to search for months. I'll get in touch in due course.'

And so in that way I had put into motion another strand of my murder investigation. I returned to the chore of packing our belongings, even though we didn't yet have a new house, but I believed in being well prepared and certainly there was a lot of household stuff that we could dispense with—changing one's home is always an incentive to clear out rubbish. During those occasional moments when I had nothing particular on my mind I gave more thought to the Murkmire Murder without troubling Bernard in the Records Office. From my point of view, there was one bonus—I knew the location very well. It was in fact the scene of the crime.

It was a remote part of the moors and while there may have been a safe route across the mire in the past, there was nothing there now. All modern routes and paths by-passed the marshy areas and visitors used that reliable network of paths because most were shown on maps. In the past, of course, maps were not readily available and people did not walk for recreation—they did so out of necessity. So I asked myself what sort of person would have trudged across those deserted heights prior to the publication of Mr Harland's book? Would the murderer have tackled a man riding a horse, for example? Or would the murderer have been riding a horse? Was that how he had evaded arrest? And why would anyone kill another human being in such a remote place? Indeed, why was the killer there at all? Did he go with the intention of ambushing or murdering the victim, or was it an opportunist crime? Or even an accident of some kind? Or the result of a feud between two local men?

The more I thought about the case and its isolated location, the more interesting it became. In my dedicated notebook I listed the sort of people who might have walked across that moor—or ridden horses there—in the years before the publication of Mr Harland's book in 1876. Much of it was guesswork, but I had to begin somewhere. I wrote down a list that included messengers, pedlars, tinkers, smugglers, itinerant merchants and dealers of various kinds including those specialising in horses. As time passed, I added minstrels, shepherds, labourers, wandering workmen, peasants out of bond, wandering preachers and friars or even pilgrims, people seeking employment or visiting relatives, outlaws, fortune tellers, quacks, herbalists, jugglers and tumblers, out-of-work soldiers, sailors going to join a ship at Robin Hood's Bay or Whitby, but after adding the word *monks*, I placed a question mark. Certainly before the sixteenth century monks would have crossed the moors regularly on foot en route between their monasteries, but after the abbeys and priories had been destroyed as a prelude to the Reformation, there would have been few if any wandering monks on those upland routes. What it all meant, of course, was that a wide variety of people would have constantly crossed that moor over the centuries—those footpaths around Murkmire would have been busy with people on the move. Even without a village or hamlet on Murkmire, there would been a constant procession of people and perhaps trains of pack-horses so was any particular type of traveller a target for robbers or murderers? Or might the killing have been done by someone seeking personal revenge? What happened to the body? Was there a pauper's burial? And I must remember that if the identity of the deceased was not known locally, he could have been a traveller—and so could the killer.

I compiled that list in the hope it might prompt a clue in my mind. One question had to be: Why would the victim have been attacked? What was the motive? Was it robbery? Was he carrying valuables and if so, what sort of people would carry valuables while trekking over those inhospitable moors? I thought very few would do so—rich people would not ride alone upon those heights. Nonetheless, anyone who was a tinker, pedlar or dealer might be carrying cash and might even be in possession of objects of use to other unscrupulous travellers. I could understand there were motives for robbery, and the isolated nature of the location meant that crimes, minor or serious, could be committed without the general public being aware of them. But murder? Could that have been concealed? Surely there would have been a hunt for anyone missing up there? But had those bogs been used to conceal the victim's remains? If so, how had the crime come to the notice of the people? There were many many questions to answer.

It would be a few days after I had embarked on this curious mission that I found myself undertaking a four hour foot patrol in Ashfordly due to the temporary absence of one of the town constables—he had to visit the dentist due to a sudden pain in his teeth—and so I was ordered to patrol the small town until routine cover resumed. I took the opportunity to check the window displays of estate agents in case there was a suitable house for sale, but none appealed to me.

Either they were too small, too large, too expensive or lacking either a garden or garage. It was a continuous exercise but I knew I must keep working at it as time was ticking away. My patrol took me around the market square and along the surrounding streets and alleys, and then I found myself passing Ashfordly Folk Museum. Immediately, my mind turned to old records and I wondered if this highly regarded museum maintained the sort of records that would be useful to my research into the Murkmire Murder. Here I might find old documents that were more locally representative than those in the County Record Office.

I went inside and found the curator, Don Wilkinson, staffing the counter. We were well acquainted.

'She's having a tea break,' he smiled as he explained the absence of the cashier. 'So is it Irene or me you want to see, Mr Rhea? I'm not in trouble so far as I am aware, and neither is she!'

'It's you I want to talk to, Don, if you can spare the time.'

'Obviously this is an official visit because you're in uniform. So I must make time!'

'It's not an official visit,' I told him. 'Although it is to do with the solving of an old murder. So it could be official business! It's old records I'm seeking.'

'Any particular orchestra or artiste? Long play or extended play?' Don had a curious sense of humour and loved putting people on the spot with such remarks.

'The local coroner,' I responded, trying to ignore his old joke. 'Going back years. Do you keep records of local inquests or court records? I'm thinking of the period before 1900 and probably going back several centuries.'

'Ah, no, sorry. You'll need the County Record Office for that sort of thing, although if someone did donate such a file to us, we would retain it if that was their wish. So what sort of inquests are you talking about? Hoards of silver or gold, or dead bodies?'

'Dead bodies. I'm trying to track down the source of the story about the Murkmire Murder.'

'Oh that! Lots of people including me have tried to get to the bottom of that yarn, and all without any results, so you'd be lucky,' he said. 'I can't remember how many have tried, lots of local authors have struggled in vain to unearth more about it. I reckon that's what it is, Nick—just a story. There's nothing to support it.'

'I think it could be one of those folk lore yarns that survives the years and gets told and re-told in pubs, getting better each time with bits added, but it must have started somewhere.'

'Yes, Nick, but where—and when? We get lots of requests for information about it but we've nothing in our files and neither has the library. In fact, I've had so many requests that I did a little research of my own, using our resources—I got nowhere apart from that vague reference in Harland's book. I'd like to do more work on it if I had time. I was going to try the County Record Office, but I'm working here when they're open.'

'I'm fortunate, I don't work normal daytime hours so I do have some free time when the Records Office is open, but the good news is that I have a slave in there right now, searching his files on my behalf, a former colleague. He's keen to delve into this case.'

'Well, the best of luck,' Don remarked. 'As I said, others have tried without success. You need something else to go on, Nick, some more information, the name of the victim or a date. It's far too vague at the moment. I must say that the more I researched it, the more I concluded it was just a tale, but I'd like to find out more. I've found no records of anyone getting murdered on that moor and with no murder, there would be no inquest. I can tell you that we have no records of such an inquest and no record of anyone being arrested. I'd say that is confirmation of the tale's legendary status.'

'It does sound very final!' I said.

'It does, but if you'd said you were interested in inquests on hoards of gold or silver, I could have shown you one of our exhibits.'

'An exhibit? Well, why not? As I'm here, I'd like to take a look. So what's special about this?'

'It came from Aidensfield, Nick. That was years ago, long before you became the local constable. I think you'll be interested so follow me.'

He raised the barrier to let me through and I offered him the necessary entrance fee, but he declined it, saying I was on official police business. As we moved into the body of the museum, his assistant returned.

'We'll be in the local history department, Irene,' he told her, and he turned me and said, 'By that I mean we won't be in folk lore, witchcraft, legends, housing, shops, herbs and so on.'

'Thanks.'

'You can get lost in here if you're not careful, it's worse than Murkmire on a dark night in a fog.'

He led me into a corner of the museum where the displays contained glass cases with artefacts discovered in old houses. He showed me a witch bottle that had been discovered under a threshold, a leather shoe dating from the fourteenth century that was found in a loft being renovated, several old coins and paintings, a God-bottle, some sturdy locks and hinges that had once secured heavy doors, crockery found in a cupboard that was being auctioned and a host of similar small items.

'All these things were discovered unexpectedly, Nick, usually during alterations or extensions to a house or during sales of household goods. But here, these are what I wanted you to see.'

He pointed to a small leather wallet-type of container that lay open and held some miniature items of silverware. Beside it was a small oblong piece of stone about the size of a paperback novel. At first, I did not appreciate the significance of either.

'Any idea what these are?' he indicated the wallet with its packed contents, all fitting in very precisely.

'It looks like a set of miniature cups, saucers and plates,' was all I could suggest. 'The sort that a child might play with.'

But I had no idea what the stone represented.

'You're a Catholic, Nick, interested in local history. That's one reason you should see these—and after my own very limited investigations, I think they could be associated with your quest into the Murkmire Murder. I stress 'could' because I have no proof, but I think a Catholic view of these plus your police experience should help. Most other people haven't go your insight. These items could be very important to you, providing just the clue you need even if I could not come up with anything. I've tried to sort it out but time's been against me. So over to you.'

He pulled a ring of keys from his pocket and unlocked the cabinet so to retrieve the silverware. He passed the items to me. 'You can take them out of the case.'

I noticed the leather case had the initials IHS on the front and recognized those as a symbolic representation meaning 'Iesus, Savour of Mankind'. There were two other initials also carved, but with less skill onto the front flap of that case, they were: JW. Then I realized what the contents were—there was a miniature chalice that could be unscrewed into three pieces, and there was also another chalice-like vessel, properly called a ciborium, that did the same, along with a patten. These were the items necessary for the celebration of Holy Mass in the Roman Catholic Church, but these small-scale examples would have been used by a travelling priest. That was the important word—travelling. A priest on the move. I hadn't included Catholic priests on my list of travellers and as Ben Tomkins had said, the victim might not have been a local man, otherwise the villagers would have known who he was.

So, even if those items could not be linked to the murder, they certainly suggested the victim could have been a priest. It certainly offered the germ of a solution. In the aftermath of the Reformation and to avoid capture and execution, Catholic priests practised their faith in secret, with many of them travelling around the countryside to celebrate Mass safely in the open air or in secret places such as private houses, farms, castles and stately homes. They were constantly being

143

hunted by the authorities hence the priests' hiding places in many large houses. If they were caught they were executed as traitors and the people who concealed them were fined or had their property confiscated. It meant that the articles they required for Mass while travelling from venue to venue had to be tiny enough to be concealed about the person should the priest be searched by a pursuivant or a parish constable.

'They're exquisite,' I said. 'These must date from the mid-seventeenth century or thereabouts? Maybe earlier?'

'We had them examined by an expert and that was her opinion, too. She told us what they were.'

'And this stone?'

'She told us about that as well. It's a portable altar stone from the same period. If you look carefully you can see five crosses etched on the face, one in the centre and the others at each of the corners. Somewhere hidden in that stone will be a relic of a martyr or saint, perhaps only a piece of hair and a fibre from some clothing. A travelling priest always took his altar stone with him, it was vital for the celebration of Mass. It had to be stone, a wooden one would not suffice. The dates of these items fit the theory that your victim might have been a travelling Catholic priest during the Penal Times—so could these have belonged to him?'

'A nice theory! How do they come to be here?' was my next question. 'And what is the connection with inquests? Are these communion items made of silver?'

'Yes they are. They were found in an old house in Aidensfield long before you arrived on the scene, Nick. It is still there and it's called Thatched Cottage, even though the roof is now tiled. It's very old and dates to the fourteenth century according to some experts and it used to have a thatched roof. Thatched with straw, by the way, not moorland ling. And then, somewhere about 1870, the owner decided to have it tiled—no doubt it had been re-thatched many times over the years, but he decided tiles were the answer. And it was while that work was being done that these items were found in a space within one of the stone walls and under the thatch.'

'Hidden?' I queried.

'Well yes, concealed by all accounts, placed in a cavity that was out of sight from the living areas. It was discovered when the thatch was removed.'

'Hence the inquest!' I smiled. 'So for some reason the coroner of that time must have decided the silverware was not treasure trove? Otherwise it would have been claimed by the state and ended up in the British Museum.'

'Exactly, it seems he decided that those tiny items had been stored for safe keeping rather than being concealed for tax reasons. And so the owner of the house passed the items to his descendants, and then recently, one of them thought they were better kept here. So we received them, fortunately. When you mentioned the Murkmire Murder, I thought you'd like to see these—I agree there is very little doubt that they came from a priest who crossed and re-crossed those moors in the seventeenth century. Your victim perhaps? So how, and indeed why, did these items get into the Thatched Cottage?'

'You've got a theory about that?'

'Yes, and there's one other small thing, Nick. Have a close look at that altar stone. See that bottom corner on the left?'

'A rusty mark, you mean?'

'It's blood, Nick, a stain we can't remove. We had it analysed.'

'Blood? So do we know who these belonged to in the first place?'

'No idea, Nick. We don't know when they were placed in Thatched Cottage, but we do know they date from the mid-seventeenth century and that the cottage was standing at that time. Those facts are not in dispute and we know the purpose of those items. A Catholic priest travelling across these moors in secret to celebrate Mass at secret venues . . . the date supports that prognosis. And that's as far as I've got with my enquiries, but I can't positively link this find with the murder. But that is blood on the altar stone.

'Human blood?' I asked.

'There's more research to do but I thought that with your police experience—and your knowledge of local Catholic history—you could take it a few stages further—especially as you are investigating the Murkmire Murder.'

'Good grief, Don, you're not honestly suggesting the dead man of Murkmire could have been that priest, are you?'

'Why not? It is something I have often considered, working here has helped me form that opinion although I've no evidence to support my theory and I've never had the time to pursue that line. That priest might have been attacked . . . it is quite feasible because he did have something worth stealing. Those silver items.'

'So his assailant must have known he was a priest even if he was in disguise? And he would have been disguised at that time, perhaps as a pedlar. No clerical collar or robes or outward signs of his priesthood.'

'True, and he might have had some cash on him, from a collection after saying Mass . . . just an idea, Nick. And if you need it, I have the names of all the occupants of Thatched Cottage from 1536 onwards and I must add that one of them was the then parish constable, a rabid anti-papist called John Reeves. His self-imposed mission was to arrest Catholic priests—it was he who arrested Father Nicholas Postgate, the Martyr of the Moors in 1678. He spent a short time living here in 1678-9, and he also served at Whitby with the Customs. You've arrived at just the right stage of this research, so it's over to you, you need to draw all those strands together. I can't do that but I can help. Let me know how you get on at the Record Office and who knows, between us we might find that killer.'

'This is incredible . . .'

With so many facts and leads arriving in such a short time I felt fate was on my side and I emerged from the museum in a state of high excitement. There was little more I could do, however, until that call from Bernard in the County Record Office. Was I putting too much effort into researching this mythical case, or had my police experience served me well, perhaps better than others who might have attempted to solve that centuries-old case? It had all been surprisingly easy so far and I wondered why others had not undertaken this research. A good deal depended upon Bernard's researches in the County Record Office and I did not wish to trouble him with more enquiries just now. After all he had promised to call me.

In fact, I had some files of my own that I had collected in my research onto the life and times of Father Nicholas Postgate. He was known as the Martyr of the Moors after his execution in 1679, but it was known he did not operate alone. He had several assistants, all priests who had entered England from the continent, and he also won the support of the moorland people, both Catholic and Protestant.

In addition I had lists of the known recusants during the Penal Times—that information was readily available in old court records even if it had never been published. And I also had the names of Catholic priests known to have been operating secretly on the North York Moors between 1536 and 1790. Again, that information was available yet successive English historians have never seen fit to publish such anti-establishment information. I wondered how much of our English history remains hidden, but in this case I felt I was making great progress.

Buoyed by this outcome, I managed to complete my tour of duty in Ashfordly without any incidents to deal with. I must admit I was preoccupied with this investigation which, in only a matter of days, had suddenly become compelling and fascinating.

No longer was it a mere legend or rumour—the tale did appear to have some basis.

It was four days later when my phone rang at 5 p.m. I was at home, having completed an early shift from 6 a.m. until 2 p.m. and it was Bernard from the County Record Office.

'Hi Nick, this is my last call of the day before I lock up. The good news is that I've found several references to

Murkmire and the murder, the bad news is that you'll have to come here to inspect the documents for yourself. I can direct you to the right areas, but there's a mass of paperwork, too much for me to wade through and only some of it is legible. So can you come here? I can have the files prepared ready for your inspection.'

'I'm on my weekly rest days next Wednesday and Thursday,' I told him. 'I could come and spend one day there.'

'Right, let's make it Wednesday at 9 a.m., then if you have to come back on Thursday, we can fit you in then. But to put your mind at rest, yes, there was a murder and an inquest, but no one was arraigned for the killing.'

Having made plans for the children to visit a friend after school that Wednesday, I persuaded Mary to have a day away from packing and cleaning. I would take her to Northallerton where I knew she would love to go shopping with a friend who lived in the town while I went off to the County Record Office to hunt through musty old papers. We arranged to meet for lunch and I said I would have Bernard with me. I owed him a meal and a pint or two.

To cut short a long story, the files gave an account of the discovery of a man's body on Murkmire Moor in March 1678. In his mid-forties, dark haired and slim, he had been dressed in the clothes of a pedlar and a pedlar's pack lay beside his remains. The murder had been investigated by a local parish constable called John Reeves and a couple of magistrates. According to their evidence at the inquest, he had died from severe head wounds inflicted by a blunt instrument that would undoubtedly have been bloodstained and the motive appeared to have been robbery because a few coins were scattered around, suggesting the assailant had fled before risking discovery. It was not known what else had been taken from the body. The identity of the deceased was then unknown and so he was buried in an unmarked grave in Aidensfield churchyard which by then had become Anglican.

It was about six months later when reports emerged of a Catholic missionary priest who was missing. He had left Grosmont Priory in March 1678. The priory had been ransacked, but a farmhouse remained, severely damaged but habitable—it was used to secretly accommodate newly arrived priests coming to England via Whitby from the continent. The missionary priest had decided to walk across the moors to Rosedale and then cross the Vale of York to the Pennines to eventually arrive in Rawtenstall, a Lancashire village close to the Yorkshire boundary.

During his long walk he had been expected to celebrate Mass in various houses along the way but he had never arrived at either Rosedale or Rawtenstall. Quite literally, he had vanished on the moors. When the alarm was raised by his supporters, enquiries commenced first at Grosmont and then at the places he should have visited en route and it emerged that his description corresponded to the murder victim on Murkmire Moor. The priest's name was James Weaver and according to the files it seemed that he had been attacked and robbed of his silver communion set. There was a possibility that there had been a tussle for possession of the silverware and that his portable altar stone may have been found and then used as a weapon.

As I studied the documents in depth, it transpired that Reeves was interrogated as a suspect due to his fanatical hatred of Catholics but a search of his house at Thatched Cottage did not reveal either the altar stone or the communion set. It was suggested, in a later document, that the killing of the priest may have been premeditated. The theft of the silver and the scattering of coins may have been done to conceal the true motive. Reeves may have successfully concealed his role as the killer but he did not dispose of the body in the bogs— to carry or even drag a corpse single-handedly across those moors would have been impossible and an attempt would have risked discovery. Another theory was that removal of the altar stone from the body, in addition to the silverware, may have been done to conceal the fact that the victim was a travelling Catholic priest and so make positive identification of the deceased almost impossible in that time of such secrecy for priests. According to the post-mortem report, the wound on the head corresponded to the corner of a stone but what had happened to his missal, rosary, chasuble and stole—all possessions of a priest? Had they been thrown into those bogs?

Reeves left the house soon afterwards and for a time worked as a customs officer at Whitby—but in leaving Thatched Cottage, he also left behind the evidence of his guilt even if it would be centuries before the hoard was discovered.

I photocopied the relevant documents for my files and then took Bernard out for lunch with Mary and her friend Rosemary. Now I knew the murder had been genuine, and we could even provide the name of the man who was surely the victim and that of his likely killer.

Next I wondered if Father Weaver's body might be found in the Anglican churchyard and re-buried in a Catholic cemetery? People whose affiliation to the established reformed Protestant Church could not be proven were usually interred away from consecrated ground and aligned north-south rather than east-west as was the custom—but as the priest would surely have been buried without a coffin, any chance of finding his remains was slight. But even without finding his remains, I felt the mission had been successful.

My next task was to visit the Brewers' Arms at Aidensfield to buy drinks for Ben Tomkins and his mates. I would now tell him my theory and vowed that one day, I would write it all down although I knew it would continue to be told as an Aidensfield folk story to frighten children and even adults away from Murkmire Moor.

CHAPTER 8

During those final weeks at Aidensfield my mind was frequently distracted from the task at hand. Both Mary and I were still trying desperately to find a suitable house and never ceased to examine all the property pages along with countless photographs in estate agents' offices. We also went house-hunting in nearby villages.

It was fortunate that I had the Chief's permission to live in the police house until my removal was complete but I discovered I would not be allowed to buy or even rent it once the closure of the beat was official. There was a mass of red tape governing the sale and rent of police property, the main rule being that it could not be sold or let directly to an individual—it had to be offered on the open market through approved estate agents after being assessed by the County Valuer.

As the date of my promotion and transfer approached with what seemed to be undue haste, I was mentally preparing to leave Aidensfield, but still had not heard anything about my proposed footpath on Aidensfield Bank. That's how things worked—you submitted a report that would require all kinds of consideration from police and county council departments such as Highways and the Treasurer and

Planning. So my report would have been copied in order that all the necessary departments could add their comments. I knew it could take a long time before even a decision to merely consider the proposal was reached.

Both Mary and I had already packed those things we thought we wouldn't require during our final weeks. As a result, our home began to look increasingly like a second-hand store. With crates, chests and assorted junk piles outside, it began to remind me of the Greengrass Farm. And in the midst of all the work, I was trying to absorb the lecture notes so that I could confidently begin my new career as an instructor in criminal law and police procedure.

That temporary comparison between my own home and Greengrass's farm reminded me that I hadn't tracked him down with his huskies and "dog cart". I decided I should make one final determined effort to locate him—after all, if I could solve the Murkmire Murder mystery, surely I could trace an ageing rogue running around the district in a "dog cart". And where was his lurcher, Alfred, while he was playing with his huskies? No one had mentioned Alfred during those sightings so had Alfred been ditched in favour of the huskies? To satisfy my own curiosity, I must find out.

Early one hot and sunny morning in June, therefore, I drove out to Hagg Bottom otherwise known as the Greengrass Farm. As on recent previous occasions, it was deserted although the hens appeared to have been fed, but his truck was absent and when I searched the outbuildings and knocked on both the back and front doors, it was evident he was not at home. The place was surrounded with mountains of assorted rubbish including old iron, household items and industrial junk and I noticed one or two cats hiding among the miasma. But Alfred had his own accommodation when he was not sleeping in the house. Familiar with the layout of the premises, I went to find him; his home was a former stable. When I reached the door it was standing open and there was no sign of the dog. Then I felt something nudging my leg—it was Alfred announcing his presence and he wagged his tail in greeting. He hadn't barked—he must have recognized my scent or footsteps. So had Alfred broken loose or did he always roam around the grounds during Claude's absence?

'Go away, Alfred,' I said at which he wagged his tail even more and came closer to be patted. I had used poacher-speak—'go away' means 'come here' while 'here boy' means 'go away.' Poachers have their own commands so that their dogs are not stolen and not controlled by other people. I looked inside the stable to see whether there were signs of him forcibly escaping, but found nothing.

I carried a dog lead in my van, an essential part of my emergency equipment, and so I fastened it to his collar without any protest and off we went. I could now use the wandering Alfred as a sort of excuse to go hunting for Greengrass. Securing the stable door, I led Alfred to the police van and he climbed into the rear without any fuss. I patted him because I did not know the poachers' words for 'good boy.'

Then I drove to the Hopbind Inn at Elsinby, one of Claude's haunts, and entered the bar, leaving Alfred in the van. The pub was not yet open for customers but George Ward, the licensee, was preparing the bar in readiness.

'Morning, George. Not bad for the time of year.'

'Hello, Nick, you're early.'

'I'm looking for Claude Jeremiah,' I told him. 'I've got Alfred in my van; he was wandering about the ranch but there's no sign of Claude.' I knew that by asking at the pub, news of Alfred's wanderings would soon be common knowledge in Elsinby and district.

'Well, you'll have trouble finding Claude nowadays, Nick. He's never at home, or hasn't been for the past few weeks, although I heard he comes back at night and goes off early next morning. He has been coming in here sometimes. But I think he does allow Alfred to wander around without being confined—he's a guard dog and Claude reckons he keeps thieves away from his business premises. Alfred's a good dog—he won't stray far.'

'If he comes in, can you tell him I've got Alfred, I'll look after him until Claude comes to collect him, I won't treat him as a stray, not just yet.'

'Aye, right. I did hear he's been spending a lot of time in Whinstone Woods, Nick—I've no idea why, I can't think of anything there that would interest him. It's not exactly poaching territory especially at this time of year.'

'Whinstone Woods?' I repeated the name because I had heard it mentioned recently—and then I recalled the occasion. 'Ah, I remember! The puma, the big cat . . . that's where it was seen.'

'Hasn't it been seen in other places?' asked George. 'I heard a rumour that a big black cat of some sort has been seen crossing a field near Thackerston.'

'So we've been told, George. Once the rumour gets under way, people will report seeing big cats all over the place. So is it a rumour set off by Greengrass to scare folks away from that wood? Is he up to something he wants no one to know about? But I'd like to know what he's doing in the wood. Now Alfred has provided me with a reason for chasing him—returning his beloved dog to him is a far better excuse than wanting to talk to him about running a "dog cart" on public roads.'

'His reason might be something to do with dogs, Nick. Huskies in particular. One of my customers said he'd seen him in Crampton with a cart and two huskies. And I can't imagine Alfred sharing his home patch with huskies!'

'I've had several reports of him being seen with a dog cart and Mrs Potiphar from Aidensfield is on the warpath because it's illegal to have dogs drawing carts on public roads, she wants me to stop Greengrass but in fact, I've really got more pressing things to do. Anyway, Alfred might help me find him quickly.'

'But huskies haul sleds, Nick, teams of them, with sleds laden down with massive loads heading for the North Pole and such . . . so why can't they haul carts on our roads? That sounds a daft law to me. Those dogs are bred to haul loads in conditions far worse than anything we can throw at them.'

'Our laws don't recognize that so I do need to talk to Greengrass about it. I've been putting it off, hoping I would come across him somewhere but he's most elusive just now. I wonder if he's keeping out of my way to follow some devious purpose?'

'All I can suggest, Nick, is that you go to Whinstone Woods and look for him there, you'll know he's not far away if his truck is parked up among the trees—but watch out for that black puma or whatever it is.'

'I will—at least I'll have Alfred to defend me!'

'He's pretty good at chasing hares, Nick, but I wouldn't guarantee he'd scare off a puma or a panther.'

And so I left George to finish his preparations for opening time. Whinstone Woods covered a large tract of boulder-strewn hillside to the north of Ashfordly. Most of the woodland comprised deciduous trees although there were a few conifer plantations. The hilly landscape the wood covered contained lots of cliff-faces which in turn had slowly eroded to produce a range of caves, large and small, that were home to a variety of wild creatures. Tumbling streams ran through lush woodland to form small lakes or ponds in low-lying areas, and the area was criss-crossed by several forestry tracks and footpaths. Those unsurfaced roads were treacherous in winter and full of pot-holes in the summer, not really ideal for motor vehicles except for those designed for forestry work.

Although owned by Lord Ashfordly, the fifty or so square miles did have some public footpaths winding their way through the trees. All of them bore notices to warn hikers not to trespass among the trees or light fires, but to remain on the public footpaths and not to camp or erect tents in the woodland. With few members of the public venturing into the woods, they were a haven for wildlife, so what was Greengrass doing there? Alfred and I might soon find out. And if anyone asked what I was doing in the woods, I could say I was hunting the puma.

During the drive to Whinstone Woods, I could not ignore the pressure to find a good spacious house and watched out for any suitable premises en route.

I needed one big enough for a family of six, close to Maddleskirk College and also within driving distance of my new posting at Solberge Hall. And, of course, it had to be within my very limited price range. I began to think I was seeking the impossible because it looked increasingly likely that I would not find anywhere suitable. But as I had to drive though Ashfordly to reach Whinstone Woods, I halted for a few minutes and I took the opportunity to check an estate agent's window, briefly leaving Alfred in charge of the police van.

I spotted a delightful stone-built, semi-detached cottage but it was marked at £6,000; it was in Maddleskirk where houses always brought good prices due to the proximity of the College. Maddleskirk was not part of my beat although I did occasionally undertake duty there in the absence of the local constable, although I hadn't patrolled there for some weeks. Maybe there was a larger house for sale? This pretty semi looked far too small for us—and far too expensive. It began to look as if the cost of a house was to be my major difficulty. My absolute limit, taking into account my salary and a few savings I'd accrued through endowment insurance, was £4,000 and even that would stretch us. What could I secure for that? Not even that tiny semi-detached house! I checked more advertisements in that agent's window, and several others but none contained anything suitable. A visit to the wood would be a pleasure!.

'Come on, Alfred, let's see what your lord and master is up to.'

And Alfred thumped his tail on the floor of the van.

Whinstone Woods lay six or seven miles out of Ashfordly and there were several entrances around its boundary, some mere footpaths over stiles but others capable of accommodating large motor vehicles.

There were parking areas too, and shelters for firefighting equipment such as hose-reels and besoms. It was rarely necessary for me to visit the woods on duty, although from time to time they were examined by the police if there were reports of poachers or ramblers camping among the trees and lighting fires. I was not very familiar with all the tracks and off-road sections of the woodland which covered a massive area so decided I would tour the main forestry routes in the hope of locating Greengrass's truck. That might lead me to him. I did not think I would encounter the supposed puma because they are shy animals and would take cover among secure cover rather than confront a human being, especially one with a dog like Alfred. I must admit I was uncertain whether or not to believe tales of its presence, but I doubted whether Claude would spend time among these trees if he was open to danger from an escaped big cat. I was aware that none of the big estates or zoos in the area had reported such an escapee, but nonetheless, the reports of sightings continued. I couldn't remember, was a puma coloured black? I knew there were creatures called black panthers which were really black leopards, their colour being a mutant form while most pumas were dark grey or a warm tawny brown, but even among pumas there could be black mutants. Or had the sightings been nothing more than a black fox or even a black fallow deer flitting through the trees?

As I drove out of Ashfordly, Alfred stood in the rear of the van, apparently interested in the passing scenery while being able to cope with all the movements such as braking and cornering without falling over or being thrown into the driving compartment. Soon we left the main carriageway to bump across some unmade tracks that skirted fields as I headed for the trees. As I entered the shade of the green canopy above, there was no sign of Claude, his huskies or his "dog cart" as I bumped my way deep into the woodland.

I could not spend too much time on a low-key enquiry of this kind but I did need to impress upon Mrs Potiphar that I had taken heed of her complaint and done something about it. And so I began a brief tour of those woods, hoping I would not get lost. Happily, the Ordnance Survey map I carried in the van did show the woodland routes and I felt I would cope.

After about half an hour of roaming the woods, and with a great sense of relief, I came across Greengrass's old truck parked in one of the spaces. I eased the van to a halt beside the truck whereupon Alfred barked in delight—he recognized the vehicle and began to whine. I decided I would remove him from the van while retaining a tight hold of the lead. But even as I was opening my door, I could see the familiar figure of Claude Jeremiah in the distance, heading towards his truck—and us—while standing in a dog cart drawn by two huskies. They were trotting along at a brisk pace with Claude standing in the cart to control them. But in those brief moments, Alfred decided to greet his master and as I opened my drivers' door, Alfred leapt out barking joyously and in that surprise he yanked the lead from my hand. He landed outside the police van and raced off to greet Claude, barking in sheer exuberance. But then there was disaster.

As Alfred tore towards Claude in his cart, his excited barking apparently terrified or alternatively angered the two huskies and they took flight, breaking from their gentle trotting motion and turning around to produce a full-blown gallop as Claude tried unsuccessfully to control them. Then they hit a pot-hole and the truck overturned to throw out Claude who landed in a bunch of nettles by the side of the track as the dogs and their cart, now bouncing along on its side, did not reduce their pace. They galloped ahead as if all the hounds in hell were chasing them, the cart bouncing along on its side as the powerful sled dogs never slackened their pace.

Alfred ignored the galloping huskies as he raced towards his master, licking him furiously and jumping up and down with excitement as Claude extricated himself from the nettle bed. Meanwhile, the huskies raced on with no sign of slacking and despite Claude's shouts to halt or slow down or mush-mush, they careered along the track and vanished from sight. By this time, Claude had struggled to his feet, his voluminous greatcoat preventing him from being severely injured or stung while Alfred showed the emotions of an untrained puppy as he excitedly fussed over his master.

And then Claude stomped towards me with absolute anger on his whiskery face. 'Now look what you've done . . . what are you doing here? With Alfred? You might have known those Eskimo Sled Dogs are terrified of Alfred, why do you think I keep them apart and why does the law have to turn up, unwelcome as usual, at this moment to create havoc and dismay . . .'

'Claude, I'm sorry, I had no idea . . .'

'Well you should have had some idea. We've got to find that cart and those Eskimos. Now. Before they really get lost. You set them off, you help to find them.'

'Yes, of course,' I felt very humble at the outcome of this meeting. 'So how do we find them?'

'Alfred's got a good nose; he'll follow their trail. But we need to keep him away from those Eskimos. And them away from him. If they get free of the cart, they'll worry him alive . . . attached to their cart, they are afraid of him so come on, Constable Rhea, we've got work to do. Right now.'

And so, with his usual heavy strides and grunting accompaniment, he began the hunt for his huskies, being led by Alfred who was tracking them with all the skill of a bloodhound.

I locked the police van and booked off the air as I trotted to catch up and soon we are heading off the main carriageway and along a narrow track with fewer pot-holes. Claude was calling the names of his huskies—then he explained to me that they weren't huskies, they were Eskimo Sled Dogs. The term huskie included several breeds of Arctic sled dogs, he told me, and as we followed close behind Alfred, Claude asked,

'Now, it's my turn to ask the questions, Constable Rhea. What are you doing here with my dog?'

'I went to see if you were at home this morning and found no one there, except for Alfred, but he wasn't locked up. So because I wanted to talk to you, I brought Alfred with me—George at the Hopbind said you were probably here in Whinstone Woods. So here I am. I thought I was doing a good turn by looking after Alfred, but sorry about that performance . . . do you think Alfred will find them?'

'Sure as eggs are eggs, yes. Now I've calmed down a bit, it won't be a problem. So what did you want to talk to me about? What have I done now?' and he grinned widely. 'Whatever it is, I didn't do it.'

'I've had a complaint from Mrs Potiphar . . .'

'Oh, her!'

'You know her?'

'Doesn't every animal-owner hereabouts know her? She does nothing but poke her nose into other folks' affairs.'

'She complained to me, officially I might add, that you had been seen with huskies drawing a "dog cart" along the public road—which is illegal, and which comes under the animal cruelty laws.'

'I know that—and it's one of the daftest laws around. But I'm not guilty, Constable Rhea. Yes, I have had my Eskimo Sled Dogs on the public highway, and I have also had my "dog cart" on the public highway, but not together. Always apart—and you know I'd never be cruel to an animal.'

'That's good enough for me, Claude. I shall tell her that.'

'Don't you know why I've been doing that? I know I'm not obliged to tell you or that woman because a fellow's private life is private, but some folks do like to poke their noses in, and not only the constabulary.'

'Go on, then, it might help to explain things.'

He told me that he had taken an interest in breeding Eskimo Sled Dogs for the English market and had joined the Eskimo Sled Dogs Society. The society held regular meetings up and down the country, sometimes with shows and demonstrations and sometimes with driving competitions. The lack of snow in England meant carts were used instead of sleds, but the dogs didn't seem to mind.

'So you see,' he said as we trudged along the path. 'Because Alfred hates the sight of those dogs, I don't keep them at Hagg Bottom. I need to keep 'em apart so I board the Eskimos out with friends, sometimes for a short stay and sometimes for longer periods, so those nosey-parkers who've reported me have seen me at various places, picking up or dropping off my Eskimos. I carry the cart around in my truck—I've a ramp to get it up into the rear. I'm in these woods because it's a good training ground for my dogs, so if I want to win an Eskimo Sled Dogs race in Edinburgh this coming winter, I need to get some training done in secret. So there we are—mystery solved. Nosey-parkers satisfied.'

'Thanks, Claude. That is just what I wanted. I can now keep Mrs Potiphar and my inspector happy. Now there's just one other thing—what about the black puma?'

'There's no such thing, Constable Rhea. Pumas are brown or mebbe grey. If it's a big black cat it might be a panther or it could be a dog or even a big furry domestic pussy cat. Or somebody might have seen something black moving in these woods—that could be a fallow deer, there some black ones in here. Or a black fox.'

'So you haven't been spreading stories about a black puma just to keep people out of these woods?'

'Would I do a thing like that, Constable Rhea,' and he blinked heavily as he assured me he would never have thought of such a scheme. 'But right now, I think we are nearing the cart and my Eskimos—Alfred's barking. So if you could take Alfred back to Hagg Bottom and put him in a shed, I'll retrieve my team and their cart. The return trip along this path will make a good training session . . .'

'Fair enough. Sorry about the fracas. And 'bye, Claude.'

'Does this mean I'll never see you again, Constable Rhea? I've heard rumours you're leaving Aidensfield.'

'They're true, Claude, but I'll see you before I go.'

And so I collected Alfred and left Claude in the woods, my first mission after returning Alfred to his home being to inform Mrs Potiphar. But could I also record the puma sightings as pure fiction? I wasn't so sure about that.

* * *

As the hours and days ticked away, I began to see my dreams were going to be shattered particularly as, in the near future, even if I couldn't find a suitable house in this area, I might soon have to find the money for school fees for all four children—not the sort of thing one does on a bobby's wage. But I plodded on full of hope and determination, and as our house-hunting continued, I began to say my farewells to the people who lived on my beat.

Over the years, I had grown to know most of them very well indeed through visiting their homes, farms, shops or inns on regular occasions. Many could be regarded as friends and for every one of them, I had the utmost respect. I could even boast a soft spot for Claude Jeremiah Greengrass.

As I toured my patch during those final weeks, I said many 'goodbyes' then Oscar Blaketon hailed me one morning as I was walking past his pub, one of several on my beat. 'Ah, Nick, a moment if you please.' I could almost hear his voice as my former sergeant saying, 'Rhea, in my office, now!' I followed him into the snug where he produced a mug of coffee and a chocolate biscuit as I settled down.

'Nick, can I ask what you and Mary are doing on the Saturday night before you start your new job?'

I opened my hands in a gesture that indicated I had no idea. 'Packing, I expect, or looking for a house or maybe just wondering what happens next. I haven't thought that far ahead. Can I ask why?'

'Well, I've looked at the calendar and July 1st is a Saturday. I know you'll not be working in your new job on a Saturday or Sunday, not at the training school—you'll start on the Monday, seeing you've landed yourself a real cushy number with no night shifts or weekend work!'

'Yes, I've been told to report there on Monday, 3rd July.'

'Which gives you all day Sunday to get over the party on Saturday night.'

'Party?'

'The people from all over your patch want to give you a farewell party, Nick, in this pub. You and Mary that is. A buffet supper, some music and entertainment or whatever. And I've also spoken to Alf Ventress and he says the lads of Ashfordly section and Eltering sub-division also want you to have a farewell do and so we thought we'd combine them. One big thrash in this pub—I will apply for an extension of hours and it means you needn't worry about driving home. That's if you're still in the police house! And, of course, you needn't do a thing—it will all be done for you. All you and Mary have to do is turn up on the night.'

'That sounds great! Yes, I'd like that and I know Mrs Quarry will baby-sit. It looks as though we'll still be in the police house, I haven't found anywhere suitable.'

'Fine, then make it a date in your diary. Eight o'clock start, finish whenever. Saturday 1st July. Your first day as a sergeant! It should be quite a celebration.'

I thanked him for the invitation and was somewhat moved to believe the residents from all 'my' villages also wanted to throw a party. I knew I'd be expected to make some kind of speech, but that would provide an opportunity for me to thank everyone for their friendship over the years and also to explain the curious circumstances when I would not be their village bobby even if I continued to live in the police house for a short while. But above and beyond all this emotion, the problem of failing to find a house was becoming a source of great stress, not only for me, but especially for Mary. We were preparing and packing to leave but had nowhere to go although I had my job to comfort me, and to provide me with a stimulus as the days raced past.

From a duty point of view during those last few days, there was one crime that threatened to spoil my 'detected' figures. It came about when Mrs Helen Radcliffe of Corner Cottage, Crampton hailed me as I was making one of my final patrols around the village on a warm summer day and saying a few farewells.

Of indeterminate age, but probably over seventy, she was a tall slender lady with an aristocratic bearing and style; she always reminded me of Queen Mary, the wife of George V.

With lots of iron-grey hair, she wore long dresses that came down her to ankles and adorned herself with pearl-like beads, bangles and ear-rings. A widow of many years, she lived in a delightful cottage near the river and the general talk was that she had been left a lot of money by her late husband who was something to do with shipping. Money did not appear to be a problem and she seemed to have enough to run a well-maintained but very old Bentley, eat at expensive restaurants and hotels, take long cruises and buy expensive clothes and jewellery. I never knew whether she had children or other family and I never saw visitors at her cottage, except friends from the locality. She seemed to entertain her friends quite a lot and in turn she would visit them, driving her beautiful old car through the lanes.

However on that morning she spotted me from her sitting-room window as I was strolling through Crampton, chatting to local people and popping into places like the shop, post office and village school to announce my forthcoming departure and leave leaflets showing how and where to contact the police in the future.

'Ah, Mr Rhea,' she emerged from her cottage looking as if she was preparing for a royal occasion. 'Have you a moment?'

'Yes, of course.'

I followed her inside where she led me into a comfortable sitting-room that reminded me of a Victorian museum piece and offered me a cup of tea with a chocolate biscuit. As it was a warm sunny morning in early summer, I noticed she did not have a fire burning but the fireplace was shielded by a floral screen. I accepted her offer and she disappeared into her kitchen while I was wondering what this was all about. Eventually she returned with a tray of goodies, placed it on a side table and smiled, 'Do help yourself, Mr Rhea, please do not wait to be asked. Now, you must be wondering why I have summoned you?'

'I hope I can be of help,' was my simple response.

'I have had thieves, Mr Rhea, or perhaps just one thief. I am humiliated because this is the very first time I have lost any of my property to thieves, housebreakers and burglars or even confidence tricksters. One does not expect such people to operate in places like Crampton. It makes one shudder to think they have been on one's property stealing one's belongings. Such actions are unforgivable.'

'Oh dear, when did this happen?'

'I cannot be sure. I would say sometime during the past three or four months.'

'That's a long time,' it was indeed a long time not to notice the loss of some goods or property. 'So what's the story?'

'Well, I never noticed my loss, Mr Rhea, it is entirely my own fault for not checking regularly and not contacting you earlier.'

'So what has been stolen?'

'Three tons of coal, Mr Rhea. Every single piece, the coal house has been emptied. I went to get some today because I have an old friend coming to stay this evening and wanted to be sure to get the house warmed and the sheets aired for her. I was going to light this fire and one in her bedroom. But when I went into my coal house just before I called you, it was empty, quite empty.'

'So when did you fill it up?'

'Before Christmas and then again at Easter. I always fill my coal house up to the limit in the weeks before Christmas, just in case we have a very long winter and cannot get deliveries. Three tons at a time, Mr Rhea. From our local coalman, Mr Wren. I enjoy good open fires so I do not stint on my use of coal, I believe in keeping my home as warm as toast. That autumn delivery lasts me until Easter, and that's when I stock up again with another three tons. That always sees me through the summer months when I don't use a great deal, and then, of course, I repeat my order to get new stocks before Christmas. I am very methodical about this, Mr Rhea, one needs to be methodical if one wishes to enjoy a calm and unflustered life. It is my Easter delivery that has gone, all three tons of it.'

'This is most odd. So can I have a look at your coal house? I need to examine the scene of the crime for my report.'

'Finish your tea and I shall show you.'

I enjoyed the tea and the chat we had about one of her cruises along the coast of Norway, and then she led me out through the kitchen to inspect her coal house. It was a traditional rural coal house where the coal was delivered either by shovel or from a sack emptied through a hatch from the side-street outside. It then slid down a short chute into the coal house. The floor was about three feet (1m) below the base of the chute and currently it was empty apart from a few odd pieces and some coal dust. There was absolutely no way a thief could have appropriated her coal by hoisting it out through that chute and hatch and furthermore the hatch was far too small for a thief to climb in, unless he was a very tiny child. So how had the three tons been spirited away? And had the evidence now been burnt?

One means of removing it was through the entrance we had used—the stable-style door that led from her house into the back garden, but that entrance was not open to the street, it was the back door of the house. The only other route to the coal house was to walk up the front garden path and around the side of the house where a high gate of solid timber formed an effective barrier. Few people came to the house by that route—most went to the front door, an unusual practice in this part of Yorkshire but that strong side-gate was usually kept locked for security reasons.

I knew that because I had visited this house from time to time. She pre-empted my comments by saying, 'As you know, I always keep that side-gate locked, Mr Rhea, always. No one could have come around the back of my house without my knowing. You can't lift all that coal out of the hatch, so how on earth has the thief managed to spirit it all away? All three tons?'

'It's a very good question, Mrs Radcliffe. Now, are you sure no one could enter your garden even when you've been away? You are away quite often,' I put to her. 'In that case, you'd not see or hear them.'

'When I'm away, I lock that gate and also lock the coal house,' she stressed, adding, 'and the greenhouse. One must be very security conscious these days. And you could not empty all that coal by lifting it over that gate, it's a very high gate, Mr Rhea, as you know, a good six feet or more.'

'And were either of those locks forced?'

'No, Mr Rhea, that's the mystery about all this. No one has ever touched those locks. Everything is exactly how it should be, except I have lost all my coal.'

'So have you noticed any pieces dropped anywhere? I think a thief making off with your coal would have dropped some of it, and besides, three tons is a mighty big load to carry off either in sacks or by the spade-full.'

'I do appreciate that, Mr Rhea, which is why this is such a peculiar crime.'

'So did you hear anything? Or see any evidence of its removal? At night in particular? I'd suggest that several trips would be required to remove it all.'

'Not a thing, Mr Rhea, and I do have very good hearing. I can hear when Mr Wren is delivering my orders down the chute so I would hear it if someone was making off with my stocks, even in the dead of night and even bit-by-bit. Bucket loads perhaps? Not only that, if anyone had spilt any on my garden paths, I would have seen it and swept it up, I do like my paths to be clean at all times. I can assure you I have not had to sweep up lumps of coal or piles of coal dust.'

While talking to her I was writing details in my official notebook and then I asked, 'Do you know if anyone else in Crampton has had their coal stolen?'

'Not to my knowledge, Mr Rhea. If someone had suffered like this, I am sure I would have learned about it, I do attend the parish church and visit the shop regularly. I do keep up to date with events in the village.'

'Well, I can support that statement, Mrs Radcliffe because I have not received any other reports either, neither here nor in any of the other nearby villages. So far as I know, this is the only theft of coal hereabouts. It is certainly a deep mystery.'

'And it is one that must be solved. So what happens next, Mr Rhea?'

'I need to make enquiries around the village, Mrs Radcliffe. I have to establish whether or not a crime has been committed here, and whether there have been other cases elsewhere.'

'But it has happened here, surely you can see that? Here am I with an empty coal house with three tons gone, spirited off in the dead of night by heaven-knows-who. So what do I do about the insurance? Will my insurance cover me for the loss?'

'It will if such a theft is mentioned in your policy, it's a case of checking with your insurance agent but the company will not compensate you for the loss until this has been officially recorded as a crime. They will check with our CID offices at Police Headquarters. That is why I must establish that this is a genuine crime.'

'Oh dear, what a performance. So I cannot claim from my insurance until all those formalities have been settled?'

'You can inform your insurance agent of the loss straight away and he will give you the best guidance about dealing with the matter, but before I submit my crime report, I must make enquiries around Crampton. I need to check with our records further afield to see if other coal-houses have been ransacked like this.'

'So will your detectives want to come and see me?'

'If I can confirm that a crime has been committed, they might send out the Scenes of Crime officers, just to check whether any clues have been left at the scene. But they will not treat this as urgent. After all, you don't know exactly when your coal was stolen, it could have happened over several weeks.'

'I did report it the moment I became aware that it had gone.'

'Yes, I know you did. There is a further problem in that we cannot differentiate between one spade-full of coal and another. Generally speaking, lumps of coal are lumps of coal without any identifying features even if they do come from different mines. If I found three tons of coal in a suspect's coal house, it would be difficult proving it had been stolen from here. But rest assured, Mrs Radcliffe, I will do my best and thankfully, the modern police service does have access to lots of resources. I will begin my enquiries in Crampton right now and it will help to know if there is a pattern to the crimes supposing other thefts have occurred, even without me being notified. I will get in touch with you as soon as I have any further news.'

And so I left her.

My instinctive feeling was that she had made a mistake about ordering her replacement load of coal—there was no way three tons could have been spirited away from her coal-shed without her or anyone else being aware of it. But I would make the necessary enquiries and first on my list was Billy Wren, the Crampton coal merchant. I called at his house on the off-chance he might be having a break for his tea or coffee, but his wife said he was delivering in Maddleskirk today. I'd find him somewhere in the village if it was urgent—if not, he'd be home around 4.30p.m.

Anxious to settle this issue I drove straight across to Maddleskirk, a journey of some twenty minutes and toured the village seeking the familiar shape of the dark green lorry bearing the logo, "Wren's Coal". I'd seen this lorry around on almost every one of my working days and found it delivering on a small housing estate. In the traditional way, Billy Wren carried the sacks of coal on his back; he wore a stout leather garment on his back while his feet were protected by large black boots with metal toecaps.

In some cases, though, he loaded his coal loose into the rear of his lorry and delivered by shovelling it into the type of chute owned by Mrs Radcliffe. Quite a lot of older houses still retained that type of coal delivery system. He noticed my arrival just as he emerged from the rear of a bungalow carrying an empty sack. I waved to ensure he realized I wanted to talk to him.

'Now, Mr Rhea. Are you looking for me?'

'I am, Billy. I need a bit of help.'

'It's here for the asking, Nick. Fire away.'

'Mrs Radcliffe of Crampton is a customer of yours, I'm told.'

'She is, indeed, a fine lady.'

'She thinks someone has stolen her last delivery of coal.'

'That would be the Easter one? Three tons?'

'Yes, that's right.'

'It's not been stolen, Nick, it was never delivered because she didn't order it. I've not seen her around to remind her. Maybe I should have dropped a reminder through her letter box, but it's not really for me to issue reminders to my customers; I don't want to be seen canvassing for orders. Really it's up to them to look after themselves.'

'I can appreciate that.'

'It's still odd, though. Obviously she's not looked inside her coal house since Easter, but she does keep a scuttle full by the hearth and a couple more in the wash-house in case she wants a fire. It means she doesn't have to go outside in the darkness.'

'Right, well she has a friend coming to stay tonight and noticed the empty coal house when she went to get some. You'd think she would have remembered not ordering it?'

'Don't be too sure about that. She used to be very good at planning ahead but she's getting on a bit now, Nick. Would you believe she's in her late eighties? And getting very forgetful. Lately she's been leaving things in the shop—she went to buy a loaf of bread last week, paid for it and left it on the counter. And she once ran out of petrol in that lovely car of hers, she'd forgotten to fill the tank one Saturday. She always topped it up on the first Saturday of the month, no matter how small the amount was but that day she forgot. There can't have been much in the tank, she must have been driving somewhere at a distance and Bentleys are thirsty brutes. She likes a really full tank, you see, just as she likes a really full coal house.'

'I get the picture, so how can I convince her she's not ordered any coal, and that her supplies haven't been stolen?'

'No one could steal coal from that place of hers anyway, not even a barrow-load let alone three tons. Look, Nick, it's partly my fault for not keeping in touch with her so leave it with me. I'll drop some off this afternoon, enough for the next few days, and then I'll have a chat before I let her have the balance. I could always be like a politician and tell a white lie by saying there's been a strike in the depot I use . . . I could say I couldn't get supplies . . . or I could tell her the truth!'

'I'll leave that to you, Billy, but I'll go and see her now to say her coal was not stolen, that there may have been an error of some sort in the delivery system! She could always check her accounts, couldn't she? I bet she's the sort of person who keeps detailed accounts.'

'She is, very meticulous. So yes, she could check the accounts. She pays by cheque, she can see whether she's issued one for the Easter delivery and I can get my wife to check our books as well, just to be certain about all this.'

I thanked him for his co-operation and then, while in Maddleskirk, I took the opportunity to seek any houses for sale. There was that small semi-detached cottage I'd noticed in the Ashfordly estate agent's window, it would be far too small—besides, the price of £6,000 was out of my reach. A quick tour of the village failed to reveal any other properties and so I returned to Mrs Radcliffe in Crampton. She admitted me with a smile, leading me into her lounge and offering me a cup of tea.

'No thanks, I must get back home,' I apologized. 'But I have some good news for you.'

'You've caught my thief?'

'Er, no, I'm afraid not. There was no thief, Mrs Radcliffe. Your coal was not stolen because in fact your Easter order was never delivered. I've checked with Mr Wren—you could check your own accounts too, to see whether you paid for a delivery around Easter. I think you'll find you didn't. Anyway, the good news is that Mr Wren will drop off a few sacks to tide you over the next few days and he'll come to see you about delivery of the balance. So all's well that ends well.'

'Well, I did have a word with my insurance man as you suggested, Mr Rhea, and he thinks my policy will cover my claim.'

'Not now it won't,' I tried to explain to her. 'There has been no crime and your coal was not stolen. It's just a case of non-delivery.'

'But when I went to my coal house the other day it was empty, Mr Rhea, totally empty, as clean as a whistle . . . someone has been taking my coal, I am sure of that. I haven't used it recently; the weather has been so mild and sunny . . .'

'All I can say is that there has been no crime, Mrs Radcliffe, and our records will show that. Mr Wren will be here soon, perhaps within the hour to drop off some coal and I will ring your insurance man tonight to explain things. Who is your insurance man?'

'It's Norman Taylor from Milthorpe,' she was not smiling now and I could see she had become rather agitated about this development. 'Mr Rhea, I am so very sorry about all this, I feel as though I am losing control of my senses, this is not the first time I have forgotten something in this way. Clearly, in view of what you say, I must have forgotten all about it. I fear my memory is failing and I hope I have not been a nuisance. Can you forgive me?'

'Of course, we all do it.'

'No, we don't Mr Rhea, it's only very old people like me, people who are going senile.'

'Don't worry, I am sure you are not going senile and even if you were, I know the villagers would look after you. If I were you, I'd be tempted to refer to this momentary lapse as a minor administrative error that has now been rectified.'

'What a good idea, Mr Rhea, how clever of you.'

And so the saga of Mrs Radcliffe's disappearing pile of coal was solved. It meant my crime figures would not show an undetected crime—I could leave my beat with a clean sheet and record this as 'No Crime.'

Now all I had to do was find a house.

CHAPTER 9

Sergeant Bairstow of Brantsford, who regularly supervised Ashfordly during the absence of the local sergeant, rang me at home shortly before I embarked on my patrol one Wednesday morning. By now, I was in the final week of my Aidensfield duties. My tenure ended on Friday—and I still hadn't found a house. I began to wonder if I'd live for ever in Aidensfield Police House.

'Ah, Nick, glad I caught you. This could be your last operational duty as the constable of Aidensfield! PC Evans, who normally covers Maddleskirk and district, has been rushed into hospital with appendicitis. He was due to interview two sisters today—they are key witnesses in a Death by Dangerous Driving case, but they've been overseas until yesterday. They're back home now. He was due to see them today because their witness statements are urgently needed, so can you go and interview them immediately? They are expecting a police officer to visit them today—they are the Misses Cotterel, Maud and Maisy. They live at Honeysuckle Cottage in the Main Street, not far from the post office.'

'I'll find it,' I'd been hoping for a quiet day free from commitments as I patrolled my beat in those final hours; I wanted to spend more time saying my farewells and hoping against hope that a suitable house would present itself to me. But taking the sisters' witness statements was not a big job—it entailed getting their version of events before committing their evidence to paper while endeavouring to eradicate any areas of doubt. And I could always have another look around Maddleskirk to see if any suitable houses had appeared on 'For Sale' signs.

I found Honeysuckle Cottage without any trouble. Built of local limestone, it was tucked into a quiet corner near the general stores. As it was set back from the road, it would be easy to walk past and never notice it.

I was quite surprised to realize that it was the semi-detached cottage I'd seen advertised in the Ashfordly estate agent's office. From the front it looked so tiny, nothing as spacious as our police house. My attention was drawn to the cottage because one of the sisters was in the front garden, weeding a borders. As I drew closer I could see the 'For Sale' sign attached to a gatepost. The adjoining semi was almost a mirror image of Honeysuckle Cottage. A long and single path led to both front doors and divided at the foot of the shared steps. A massive honeysuckle plant grew against the front wall between the doors and formed archways over both. The doors were painted in the same royal blue and the Yorkshire sliding windows of both cottages looked crisp with a recent coat of paint. The houses were like twins and stood peacefully on a patch of land just off the main street. If one was Honeysuckle Cottage what was the other's name? Nos 1 and 2 Honeysuckle Cottage perhaps?

'Miss Cotterel?' I asked.

'Ah, yes, I am Maud. My sister is inside. Do come in, we were expecting you, Constable.' She was a tall and slender lady with silvery white hair drawn back from her face and she spoke with a refined accent. Her eyes were a beautiful sky blue and she had a nice smile too. I liked her immediately. She began to lead me towards the house.

'I'm PC Rhea from Aidensfield,' I introduced myself. 'PC Evans has been taken into hospital with appendicitis so I am deputising.'

'Oh, dear, how dreadful for him. I hope he makes satisfactory progress,' and she led me along the path and towards the blue door on the left of the pair. 'Welcome to our modest home.'

'I see your cottage is for sale,' I commented as we approached the front door.

'I wish we could get a buyer,' she said, pausing outside for a moment or two look across the garden. 'We've committed ourselves to another property in Eltering, but this one stubbornly refuses to find a buyer. In fact, we've reduced the price considerably.'

'I saw it advertised in Ashfordly,' I said. 'I must admit I thought it was rather highly priced for a semi-detached cottage.'

'Semi-detached? But no, it's not a semi, Mr Rhea. This is one large house—it is two good cottages knocked into one. Those two front doors do confuse people, I'm afraid, but there are also two back doors leading into the garden—that's most useful—and we have four large bedrooms, a bathroom and toilet, a utility room, two lounges and a good kitchen. And a large garden behind the house which is secure, ideal for children at play. There is even a strongly constructed swing in the garden, and a lovely old stone shed, a former blacksmith's smithy and stable. We still find old horseshoes when we're gardening. If only people would come and look around instead of relying on photos, it would be a good thing. They'd see for themselves.'

'Good heavens, I had no idea! I thought it was two cottages. That's how it appears on the photo, the one in the estate agent's in Ashfordly.'

'So are you looking for a house, Mr Rhea?' She had quickly recognized my interest.

'Yes, I am,' I said, and my heart began to pound as I explained the reason for my house-hunting while outlining the sort of accommodation I would need for two adults and four children.

'Even so, I couldn't afford it,' I admitted. 'The estate agent's notice says the price is £6,000.'

'Oh, we were badly advised on that, Mr Rhea, it is a silly price. We've come down a lot since then, down to something much more realistic so I am surprised that the old price is still being advertised. The agent was told of our new price before we went away, the adverts should have been amended. I'm surprised they haven't been. There is little wonder we've had such a poor response.'

'Well, it was showing that price the other day and there's nothing to indicate the property is a detached house created from two cottages.'

'I think the estate agent wants someone to go along and make an offer, then he has scope to reduce the price. We don't agree with those tactics—we feel we should advertise it at a reasonable price that will attract a buyer. House prices have fallen so much in recent months as I am sure you know. I must speak again to those agents; they must make it clear that this is a single house at a much reduced price.'

'So what is the actual price?'

'£4,000,' she said. 'We think that is much more realistic—after all, there is no central heating, no garage and this is very old house with no damp course. And you need to look at the roof . . . it sags a lot. People always comment on our roof, but it is solid and doesn't leak.'

'It looks most charming,' I smiled. 'A rustic roof on a proper rustic cottage!'

'We like it like that too. We were advised never to attempt to upgrade the roof or to touch it in any way, otherwise we'd have problems. Leave it like that, we were told, it's been like that for centuries and will probably last for centuries more.'

'I could afford that price, and the accommodation sounds suitable,' I heard myself say. 'But I'd need to talk to my wife . . .'

'By all means bring her along when you have a moment and she can see what we've got here. I'll show you round the house and garden before you leave.'

And so it was that in a state of some excitement I took the necessary witness statements from both sisters. Each spoke fluently and each had a clear, but quite distinct version of the events they had witnessed. Each supported the account provided by the other. I wrote down the statements in long-hand on the forms used for such matters and obtained their signatures as required. I would get those statements into the post as soon as possible—no later than today's last post in fact.

But the sisters, both equally charming, insisted on showing me around before I left. The house was charming—and ideal for my family. The date of construction was unknown but it had a York range in the kitchen complete with fire-side oven, old oak beams, thick walls, Yorkshire sliding windows, a narrow, twisting staircase with a cupboard beneath, bags of character and lots of cupboard space plus that wonderful honeysuckle around its two front doors.

No one was quite sure when the two cottages had been knocked into one, but the central wall was about three feet thick and built like a fortress. All the rooms were spacious, including the bedrooms—the smallest could be a single room for Charles, there was a larger room for Elizabeth with the other girls sharing the largest bedroom. That room could be divided with a partition and there was a double room for Mary and me. There was also a bathroom and separate toilet upstairs. With three reception rooms and kitchen downstairs, I could have a study of my own—a necessity for my writing ambitions! As I wandered around in something of a daze, I knew this place had all the requirements I needed. Except a garage. But when examining a house with a view to purchase, one always gets a certain feeling that something is right—and that's what I immediately felt about Honeysuckle Cottage.

In spite of its drawbacks—no garage, no damp course, no central heating and a sagging roof—I knew this could be our picturesque new home.

The lack of a garage was no problem—Maud and Maisy each had a car and rented garages from a farmer just across the street. That tenancy—for two cars—could be passed to the new owners of Honeysuckle Cottage. Much later into the negotiations, my parents said they would help with the installation of central heating—and so I was left with no damp course and a sagging roof, both of which, it seemed, had deterred other potential buyers. The damp course could be treated and the sagging roof was weather-proof. When Mary saw the house she loved it. The kitchen was spacious with its black-leaded York range and an open fire; the ancient beams had clothes-drying rails hanging from them, along with bacon hooks and huge bolts whose purpose was obscure—all relics from a past way of life.

The garden was about a third of an acre, mainly down to lawn, but there was a strawberry patch, soft fruit bushes, apple and plum trees, and an area for growing potatoes and other vegetables. There was also a hen run with a wooden henhouse, and a stone building that had formerly been a blacksmith's stable that accommodated waiting horses.

We quickly decided we should make an offer but first had to speak to a solicitor and our bank manager, promising the Cotterel sisters we would keep in touch. Within a day or two we made a formal offer of £4,000.

And then the problems started. As we made desperate attempts to sort them out, time was ticking away. We approached several building societies for a mortgage but when their surveyors saw the sagging roof, they declined to make an offer. I lost count of those we approached and the bank could not help—at that time they did not lend money for mortgages.

Then a friendly solicitor living on my patch—(not our solicitor by the way)—hailed me and said, 'I've heard from the Cotterel sisters you're having difficulty getting a mortgage on Honeysuckle Cottage?'

'It's the sagging roof,' I explained. 'The surveyors take one look at it and refuse to make any kind of offer.'

'Try the Scarborough Building Society,' he suggested. 'Their surveyor likes old houses.'

And so I did. He was the only surveyor to actually climb into the roof void. Once inside the loft, he tested the timbers and the strength of the joists, poking and tapping as he moved about above the bedrooms. Certainly, that old roof was not underdrawn and it was possible to see daylight between the pantiles, but it had never let in water or snow. There was no dampness or rot in the roof space, and the timbers were not affected by woodworm. And so his society made an offer. But it wasn't enough! Due to the age of the house, it was only 80% of their valuation, not the usual 90% offered on most houses. Fortunately, they valued it at £4,000—the mortgage offered would therefore be £3,200.

It meant, with all my savings I was still £400 short of the necessary funds. £400 between me and my own house! It seemed like an unbridgeable chasm and the bank couldn't help any further. I'd already stretched myself to the limit and beyond with agreed borrowings and had no wish to tempt loan sharks or take out other loans on top in addition to everything I needed to buy the house such as a second car and legal expenses. If I borrowed any more, the interest rate would be crippling and I'd not be able to meet my repayments or overheads. It was with immense sorrow, therefore, that, after all the euphoria and excitement, I went to see the Cotterel sisters.

'I can't raise the money,' I admitted with some shame, explaining the problem in considerable detail. 'We'd set our hearts on Honeysuckle Cottage, it's just what we want but with all the expenditure involved and the offer from the mortgage company, we're still £400 short.'

'We'll lend it to you,' said Maud with no hesitation. 'Repayable over ten years with no interest. Forty pounds a year. That's less than a £1 a week. Will that help?'

I could have thrown my arms around her and kissed her.

And so we bought Honeysuckle Cottage.

The fact that I had informed my superiors that we had submitted an offer for the purchase of Honeysuckle Cottage meant that the official wheels began to turn, even though the deal had not been finalized. What happened next was that I received a telephone call to say an official from the County

Architect's Department would arrive to examine Aidensfield Police House for the purpose of compiling a suitable advertisement for its impending sale.

For me, that was adequate confirmation that the beat was to close upon my departure—the police house was soon to become surplus to requirements. In due course, the official arrived. By the name of Alex Dunbar, he was a young man with a mop of unruly blond hair and a rather crumpled suit, but he was pleasant enough as I conducted him around the police house. He made copious notes on a pad of official forms adding that this house had been constructed before he had commenced his career with the County Architect's Department, and so he was unfamiliar with its construction and layout. But he did say its specification was high and it had been well built.

'Nice views too,' he added as we toured the garden.

'You can see Fylingdales Ballistic Missile Early Warning Station from here,' I said, pointing out what I thought was a good selling point. 'And there's that wide view of the dale below. Lovely in summer, but more than a bit blustery in winter, in fact it's like living in a wind tunnel at times.'

I decided that I should mention that the wind was so strong that at times the rugs in the hall floated on air like magic carpets and moved around the floor as the wind found its way through gaps and cracks in the doorway. There were times when the gales were so powerful that I could not open my garage doors. If I did succeed in opening them, I could not anchor them in the open position because the power of the wind overcame the capacity of the bolts that held them open. And so the doors slammed shut. They behaved like the sails of a schooner and there were times when I wondered if the house would begin to turn on its axis, so powerful were the gales. But the house was surprisingly well built despite a few defects—Mr Dunbar said they could be remedied quite easily.

After his examination he said it might require some upgrading before the sale, such as a new central heating system and better-fitting windows, but he felt it would sell very quickly. It would attract interest because it was a stone-built detached house with a matching garage and set in its own grounds on a hilltop site. There was plenty of privacy with magnificent views over the dale and across to the moors. And it had an office attached.

'So you're not buying it?' he asked.

'No, it's too small for my family. I've got four growing children so we need something with more space and extra bedrooms. Apart from that, we need something soon, and buying a police house can take ages due to all that red tape.'

'Well, once all our formalities are concluded, and the powers-that-be agree on a price, we'll put the house on the market. I agree that might take some time. But we will not go for completion while you are still living here, of course; your chief constable has explained his promise that you can stay for a short time until you've secured your own property.'

'Yes, that was most consideration of him.'

'He's a nice man and a good boss. Now, PC Rhea, we do appreciate that this is an operational police house which means you are away from it for most of your working hours and so we shall make viewing by appointment only. Anyone wishing to view the property will be accompanied either by me or a member of my department. I will keep in touch with you as time goes by, but very soon we shall come to erect the 'For Sale' signs which will coincide with advertisements in the local paper. But you might have left by the time we begin to get serious offers.'

As Mary and I worked on our packing and planning, a man arrived with the 'For Sale' signs and erected one in the garden by the attached office, and another at the other end of the property, near the garage. The name and details of an estate agent were included along with a clause to stress that viewing was by appointment only. I must admit I wondered what would happen to the carved stone police badge that was built into the wall of the office, but that was not my problem. I did not want it and had no wish to incorporate it in the wall or garden of Honeysuckle Cottage. It was far too big to be a useful ornament and apart from that, I had no wish for people to call at my new home in the belief it was a police house.

Things were now happening with surprising speed and then one morning as I was preparing to begin my routine patrol, the bell on the office door sounded and I went out to see who was there. It was Claude Jeremiah Greengrass.

'Come in, Claude, this is an unexpected pleasure.'

'Now there's no need to be sarcastic, Constable Rhea. Not come at an inconvenient moment, have I?' he beamed. 'Not got you out of bed or disturbed you in the middle of having your porridge? Or would it be eggs and bacon? Or champagne and salmon with scrambled egg?'

'No, Claude, nothing like that. I've eaten my fill and am ready and fit for anything.'

'Even me,' he chuckled.

'Even you and even at this time of day. So what can I do for you?'

'I've heard your house is coming up for sale, I knew you were leaving but this makes it pretty final, doesn't it? Selling the house, I mean.'

'The beat is being closed, Claude. It's all part of progress.'

'Backward progress if you ask me. I know we've not always seen eye-to-eye but you've allus been fair and you've had a job to do. Not the easiest of jobs, I know, but it won't be the same without a constable on the hill.'

'There'll be teams of other constables patrolling the area,' I explained. 'It'll be just the same but with different faces in those uniforms.'

'Aye, but you kept an eye on my yard, making sure folks didn't come and help themselves to my valuable commodities. I got personal attention. And Alfred likes you. He doesn't like many men in uniform, just you ask the postman. Things like that are appreciated, I can tell you, and I know you'd help me if I really needed it. Like I would help you if you were in trouble. We're mates, Constable, good mates.'

'Yes we are Claude, it's kind of you to say so, I appreciate it.'

'Aye well, there's allus change in the air but it won't be easy, making pals with the new coppers and learning whether I can trust 'em. Any road, I'll do my best to behave but that's not why I'm here. It's about this house sale.'

'What about it?'

'How do I go about making an offer? Who do I talk to? Is it you?'

'You, Claude? You want to buy this house? Are you serious?'

'I wouldn't be here if I wasn't serious, would I? It's not often I come voluntarily to the police house, is it? I'm usually here under protest.'

'Well, I must admit it's pleasing to see you so you'd better come in and Mary will make us a cup of tea or coffee.'

'Coffee for me, two sugars and milk,' was his swift response.

And so I led him into my office and settled him down as Mary organized the drinks. There was a bit of banter between them but all on a friendly basis and it was then I realized I would miss Claude Jeremiah Greengrass and all his schemes. Life wouldn't be the same without him.

'Nice office,' he was looking around as if contemplating the place for some specific purpose. 'Plenty of room, light and airy, night-store heater, counter and shelves. Aye, this would make a very nice office.'

'You've got plans for the house, have you?'

He touched the side of his nose with his forefinger, as if to say, 'Mind your own business,' then continued, 'So what's upstairs?'

'Two large bedrooms, one small one like a boxroom, a bathroom and separate toilet. And downstairs, a dining room next to this office and a lounge next to it, both with southerly views. A kitchen, a downstairs toilet, a washroom and a cross passage. And a garage beside a very large garden. Highly desirable, Claude. I'll show you around after coffee.'

'I'd like that. So who do I see about making an offer?'

'The estate agent is listed on those signs outside.'

'Can you put a word in for me? You know, as an old mate, a man of good character and sound business acumen, the sort who'd make a splendid occupant of a former police house.'

'I'm not allowed to do that, Claude, the house is not mine to sell, and at the moment it is still official police property. There are official channels to negotiate if you want to put in an offer. And I am not allowed to give references to anyone.'

'Well, I am sure you'll not say decog— derog— decogoratory . . . er, remarks, er, I mean nasty things about me.'

'Of course not.' And so we sat for a few moments with our coffees as I was dying to know why he was so interested in the police house. But he was giving nothing away.

I began to wonder whether this was some kind of joke or whether he was truly serious in wanting to buy the house. In the absence of the man from the County Architect's Department, I showed him around the accommodation both upstairs and downstairs, and he seemed very pleased with it. Not surprisingly, he noticed that the kitchen was very small, but suggested he could demolish the inner wall to create an extension into the lounge to make a larger living area and kitchen combined. He also felt the bathroom was rather too tiny to accommodate his bulk.

When we had finished, he said, 'Right, Constable Rhea, thank you for your hospitality and kindness. I'll be in touch if I want another look around but I will contact the estate agent later today.'

'So how's the new enterprise coming along?' I asked as he was leaving. 'Your breeding of Eskimo Sled Dogs? And sled racing?'

'I've decided not to go down that road,' he said. 'Alfred's the main reason. He would never allow Eskimo Sled Dogs to live at Hagg Bottom and it isn't easy finding alternative accommodation for them, not everyone wants that kind of dog on their property. So I've given it all up. I might still go to their shows though.'

'Fair enough, it sounds like a sensible decision. So what about that puma?'

'I've never clapped eyes on it though, but I'll tell you what, there's a chap camping in those woods. I saw his smoke and then Alfred found him in a cave and barked, so I went along for a look.'

'So who was he? A hiker?'

'No, one of the monks from Maddleskirk Abbey, he's trying to live like a hermit but he won't find it easy, not in those woods even if folks do bring him offerings and alms and clean socks. I reckon that's what folks have seen—he wears a black habit and if he was flitting silently between the trees, folks might think he was a ghost or a black deer or even a puma. It's amazing what you find in our woodlands, Constable. Probably more than monks and pumas.'

'I couldn't agree more, Claude.'

And off he went without leaving any kind of explanation about his plans for the police house. As I watched him drive away in his battered old lorry, I wondered what on earth he was planning to do with my former house. Not knock it down to build another? Use the land for his livestock? Turn the house into a holiday cottage? Make it his main home and use his existing ranch as his business depot? Then he could let his present house as holiday accommodation—I was sure some people would love to spend their holidays among all his assembled junk, muck and pungent pongs.

Before I left to undertake my planned patrol, Mary came through to clear away our mugs. 'Did he come to say good-bye?' she smiled.

'No, he says he wants to buy this house. I don't suppose there's anything to stop him although I've no idea what the planning people would think if he wants to turn this into his business premises or a junk yard or smallholding or something similar.'

'I can't believe he's serious! He's doing this just to annoy you, Nick, you know what he's like.'

'I got the impression he was very serious about it, so all we can do is wait and see what happens next.'

With the 'For Sale' signs in position and adverts appearing in the local press, there was a lot of interest in the police house. People came from far and wide to view the premises, many of them abiding by the 'By appointment only' condition. Nonetheless, some did ask for a look around because they were from a distant town or village and were merely passing through—their excuse was that they wanted a general impression of the house before deciding whether to proceed with serious offers. On occasions I did pop into the estate agent's office to see how things were progressing, but my discreet enquiries showed there had been no offer from Claude Jeremiah Greengrass and he had not even been into the estate agent's office to collect a brochure. I began to think it was all one of his jokes.

Then one of the neighbours who lived only fifty yards or so away from the police house hailed me outside my house. It was old Mr Atkins, a retired farmer who was in his mid-eighties.

'Now then Mr Rhea,' he was always very formal. 'What's all this about Greengrass buying your house?'

'I think it's just a rumour he's spreading around. You know what he's like, more than a bit devious.'

'That's not according to what I've heard, Mr Rhea. I've heard tell he knows somebody with pots of money who wants to turn it into an expensive gambling establishment—enlarge the buildings, gut the interior to make it into one large casino with roulette wheels and blackjack, bedrooms upstairs, offices downstairs and plenty of car parking space not to mention mood music, dancing and bars. Think of the disturbance to us folks living nearby.'

'They'd never get planning permission for that! Not on Aidensfield hilltop,' I couldn't believe what I was hearing. 'Who told you that?'

'It's all around the pubs in here and Elsinby. I bet Claude's behind it.'

'Thanks, I'll make enquiries but I would like to see whether that is a feasible idea. If it's what Greengrass is telling everybody, I think we should take it all with a pinch of salt, Mr Atkins.'

'You can't trust that man, Mr Rhea, not a single inch.'

'I don't know what he's up to but even if he or an acquaintance bought the house, they'd never get planning permission for that sort of thing no matter how rich they were—besides there are very strict legal rules about premises used for gaming. I know the gaming laws are soon to change but that's a year or two away. I reckon he's been spreading malicious rumours.'

As a precaution I rang Mr Dunbar in the County Architect's Department and he was adamant that such a scheme would never be approved, and he added he had never had any requests for information from Claude Jeremiah Greengrass. The old rogue was clearly up to his usual mischief-making self and I couldn't understand why he was doing so.

Then I heard another rumour the house was going to be turned into a discreet small cinema with an attached restaurant. Once I realized that these rumours emanated from Claude, it was clear he was up to something, so I thought I'd turn the tables on him, but most discreetly. It would be several days later when I went to the village post office just as Claude was emerging.

'Now then, Constable Rhea,' he breezed up to me in the street. 'Sold that house of yours yet?'

'Just about,' I smiled. 'Things are going well. It looks as though we've got a buyer but keep that to yourself, it's confidential at the moment.'

'You know me, Constable, my word is my bond. Not a whisper will I make to anyone. But is it a serious offer? I'm still interested in buying, you know,'

'It's a couple of racing pigeon experts from Skinningrove, they want to turn it into a huge pigeon loft. They reckon that hilltop site is ideal for racing pigeons and homing pigeons or whatever they are called.'

'Racing pigeons? You're joking!'

'I'm not, Claude. It's perfect, according to them. No obstructions, right on a hill top with no dangers from pylons, forests and so forth. Completely open, ideal for landing and taking-off. There's plenty of room for both a house and the lofts. Apparently planning consent won't be a problem either, the birds aren't noisy apart from a spot of billing and coo-ing so they won't upset the neighbours.'

'But a pigeon loft?' he shouted. 'You can't be serious!'

'It's out of my hands, Claude, as I explained earlier. But I think it will make an ideal loft—all that space, that eleva-tion, a quiet location, a good landing and take-off site . . . have you seen those lofts in Skinningrove? They're very sim-ilar to the design of this police house. House and lofts would look fine together.'

'I've never been to Skinningrove in my life,' he mut-tered. 'I've no idea where it is . . .'

'Not far from Loftus and Saltburn, on the coast,' I told him. 'Very important pigeon country.'

'Why would I want to go to see a pigeon loft?'

'There aren't any around here, except in stately homes but they're a different sort of thing, Claude, there they're called dovecots. They were used for breeding doves for food. Lofts are for racing pigeons, as I am sure you know . . .'

'You're not telling me anything new, PC Rhea, except that I can't believe anyone would want to turn that house of yours into a pigeon loft.'

'You'd be surprised what some people do with the houses they buy.'

'I don't think I would be surprised at anything anymore. Pigeon loft . . .' and he stomped away muttering to himself. 'No one keeps pigeons around here . . .'

It wasn't long before the pigeon loft rumour executed a full circle and returned to me in an expanded and much enhanced version, this one being that an international consortium of pigeon fanciers was going to develop the police house into a central control point for recording all aerial pigeon movements, both during training flights and in races, rather like the control tower in an international airport. I did nothing to correct the notion and there's little doubt that the villagers did not quite know what to make of these developments. I am sure some realized they were all expansive rumours not founded on fact but there is no doubt some took a very serious view of the uncertainty.

Letters appeared in the papers expressing concern at the departure of the village constable with a plea that whoever bought the redundant house would promise not to disturb the traditional peace and tranquillity of Aidensfield hilltop.

In the meantime, however, my bid for Honeysuckle Cottage was being processed and it was not long before I received confirmation from the Scarborough Building Society that my application for a mortgage had been approved, and I could proceed to completion. I rang my solicitor and Mr Dunbar from the County Architect's Department to let them know I was now in a position to proceed with my purchase of Honeysuckle Cottage. My solicitor said he'd set a date for completion. Likewise, I informed the Superintendent so that he could notify the chief constable and set the official police wheels in motion.

While talking to Mr Dunbar, I took the opportunity to ask whether any serious buyers had made bids for the police house and he said, 'Yes, we've one very serious applicant. In fact, he has made an offer in excess of the asking price and we are proceeding with that. He does not require a mortgage and is seeking a rural location. He has a relation living near you—a man called Claude Jeremiah Greengrass.'

'Now that is amazing,' and so I told Mr Dunbar about the rumours that had been circulating about the forthcoming use of the house.

'We were aware of those, Mr Rhea, we think your Mr Greengrass deliberately set the rumours off to try and dissuade local people from wanting to buy the house, he gave the impression that the proposed buyers had more than enough money to ensure they got exactly what they wanted. I don't think his plans worked. No one would believe such tales. But then we heard it was going to be used as a pigeon loft . . .'

'So who is the proposed buyer?' I butted in rather rudely. 'Am I allowed to know?'

'No names, Mr Rhea, but he is a market gardener who wants to open a specialist garden centre on that site, growing and dealing in alpines and such, hardy flowers that thrive in the northern hemisphere. He wants to catch the passing trade and so car parking might cause him some planning difficulties although there is plenty of space, but he reckons his plans are feasible and also reckons the south-facing slope of the police house garden would be ideal as a vineyard.'

'A vineyard? Are you serious?' I asked.

'He reckons the earth and climate equate with some of those in the south of France, but time will tell,' was all he would say.

And so my planned move into Honeysuckle Cottage headed inexorably towards completion. The entire exercise took a further few weeks even though I did not have a house to sell. The fact that the Misses Cotterel had already bought another property helped to speed things up, but none-theless there were lengthy formalities and legal matters to pass through slow-moving solicitors. However, everything was very positive which eventually meant I could give for-mal notice to the chief constable that I would be vacating Aidensfield Police House on Friday, 7th July. In the mean-time, I had contacted several removal firms to obtain quotes and found the cheapest came from the same company that had moved me into the Police House all those years earlier.

Had I been moving from one police house to another on an official transfer, I would have been granted three days leave in which to move—one before the date, one on the date and one the day following—but because I was moving into my own premises I did not qualify for that allowance. Happily, my boss at the training school, Chief Inspector

Langton, understood the problems of moving with a young family and gave me that Friday off duty.

'We've guest lecturers coming in every Friday, Nick, so take the day off. It'll give you Saturday and Sunday to get yourself sorted out.' I thought that was a most encouraging start to my new job.

Before we left Aidensfield, we attended our farewell party in Oscar Blaketon's pub; it was a lovely evening and everyone—police colleagues and villagers alike—had contributed towards a present for us, chosen particularly with Mary in mind. Policemen's wives tend to get forgotten at times—but not Mary. She was a keen gardener and, because there was almost a third of an acre for cultivation at Honeysuckle Cottage, we found ourselves presented with a range of gardening tools and equipment. It included a spade, fork, rake and new wheelbarrow!

'The tools are for both of you, Sergeant,' said Oscar Blaketon, emphasizing my new rank as he made the presentation on behalf of everyone. 'You'll have much more spare time now you're working normal hours with no nights or weekend duty. I can see you catching the gardening bug!'

I took the hint . . . I was never much of a gardener. If I planted potatoes or beans or carrots or other household vegetables, the slugs and other creepy-crawlies enjoyed them long before we had our turn. But the stainless steel tools would be wonderful for Mary! She was very keen to have her own garden and we both thanked everyone most sincerely. In all seriousness, however, the presents might encourage me to take a greater interest in the mysteries of growing vegetables or nurturing flowers and shrubs.

On the day of our move, the children went to school knowing they'd never return to their old home and as if on cue, the moment they'd gone, the furniture van appeared. It eased to a halt outside our gate and two men got out. I went to meet them.

One was rather squat with several days' growth of beard—he was the driver—and his companion was the tallest and thinnest man I'd ever seen. These were the same characters who had moved me into the Police House about five years earlier.

'Now then,' said the driver.

'Now then,' said his thin companion.

'Good morning,' I returned.

'I see you've still got that same narrow gate,' observed the driver.

'You've got that same narrow gate,' repeated the thin one.

'It was replaced by the insurance company after you'd knocked it down last time,' I reminded them. 'It's as good as new.'

'You'd think they'd have made it wider while they were at it, wouldn't you? But they never do. We reverse our truck into t'space, knock down t'gate because it's too narrow and they allus replace it just as it was. We've moved every new bobby into this house and out again over the years and we've allus knocked t'gate down. They've allus put it back just as it was. That's summat I can't fathom. Why don't they build wider gates? I'll never understand insurance companies.'

'We'll never understand insurance companies,' said the thin one.

'So you're going to knock it down again?'

'Aye, we need to get our truck as close as we can to t'house, and off t'road. But t'insurance will pay, good thing insurance, really.'

'Good thing insurance really,' chipped in the thin one.

'Have you still got that bloody piano?' asked the driver.

'Yes, I have,' I replied with a feeling of impending doom. My handsome ebony piano, a twenty-first birthday present from my parents, was a mighty and excessively heavy iron-framed monster with a grand piano keyboard.

Its journeys around the North Riding during removals in the course of my police duty had caused untold headaches both to me and to those who tried to manhandle it into or out of our various houses. On one occasion, it was placed on the tarmac footpath outside a house into which we were moving, and it was so heavy all four wheels sank into the surface. It had to be prised out of its resting place. On most occasions, various household doors had to be removed to allow the huge instrument in and out of the house . . . and it seemed history was about to repeat itself. I began to dread this latest removal—it was made worse because I had never learned to play the piano.

'It'll mean taking that front door off its hinges,' said the driver.

'We'll have to take that front door off its hinges,' said the thin one.

And so, in a slow motion re-play of my arrival at Aidensfield, they boarded the lorry, reversed into the gate, smashed down both posts with their rear bumper followed by a splintering of wood as they manoeuvred the vehicle as close as possible to the house, leaving indented wheel marks across the lawn.

'We might as well take that door off its hinges now if that piano's got to come out,' said the driver.

'We'll take that door off its hinges now,' said the thin one.

In the weeks before the arrival of the van, both Mary and I had done a lot of preparatory work, she packing the crockery, glassware, ornaments, toys and such in tea-chests and cardboard boxes. I had demolished wardrobes, beds, dressing tables and kitchen units. Moving regularly around the county, our furniture had been taken apart on countless occasions and I was very adept with a screwdriver, hammer and pliers. In fact, some of our belongings never got unpacked—boxes with mysterious and forgotten contents were often long-term residents in police officers' lofts.

I must admit I wondered if the piano could be taken apart into manageable sections, but felt that was beyond me. I must admit I began to wonder if it could be manhandled into Honeysuckle Cottage. And would I ever learn to play it there?

The doors and passages of Honeysuckle Cottage were very narrow and awkwardly located. I groaned as I wondered what these men would say when they saw the cottage and how they would deal yet again with this troublesome piano. While they worked at Aidensfield, Mary kept them going with constant cups of tea and biscuits and I must say they worked very hard and rapidly and without complaint; they were clearly keen to get the job finished so they could finish early. One blessing was that our new home was only a couple of miles from Aidensfield police house. It was not as if we were moving from one end of Yorkshire to another.

By lunchtime, our meagre belongings were all onboard—and with the aid of a small trolley and thanks to the temporary absence of the front door, the removal men had steered the piano out of the house and somehow managed to get it up the ramp into the removal van. Compared with last time, extrication of the piano had been surprisingly simple. The men took their lunch in the van while we had sandwiches and a flask of coffee that Mary had prepared. Then she drove along to Honeysuckle Cottage to oversee the arrival of the furniture and allocate rooms for boxes and so forth, while I remained to clean up and secure the police house.

It would require a more thorough cleaning, but meanwhile I could check that everything of ours had been removed and that all the fixtures and fittings in both the police house and its adjoining office were *in situ*. There were more formalities than expected when moving in and out of police accommodation, but at this point it was merely a case of checking a printed form and ticking various boxes.

Of course, I would have to record the damage to the gateposts and lawn with a note that the removal firm's insurers would pay, as always. Fortunately there was no other damage—they had not dropped or broken anything belonging to us.

Mary had left in her car before the removal men had finished their lunch break and we had earlier arranged for the children to walk straight from school into the new house.

They could help unpack the boxes destined for their own rooms while I remained to complete my formal chores. It would take me about an hour to complete all the necessary odds and ends.

When Mary and the removal men had gone, I felt an unaccountable twinge of emotion as I stood alone in the deserted house that had been both my home and office for about five years. We'd been very happy here—Mary had loved the village and its people and she'd made a lot of friends even if she was forever known as 'the policeman's wife'. The children had liked the open spaces on the moors and around the village. They'd even loved their village school and had made friends there. Throughout my beat, I'd met delightful people and my work had been totally fascinating and emotionally rewarding. Being the constable of Aidensfield had been a happy and memorable part of our lives. With more than a hint of a tear, therefore, I went inside the deserted house to finalize checking the inventory and to record my departure, my final duty as the constable of Aidensfield. As I moved around the echoing rooms, however, the doorbell rang. When I answered, I found Claude Jeremiah Greengrass standing there.

'Your missus said you were still here,' he said with his hands hidden behind his back.

'Hello Claude. I'm just finishing off a few chores,' I said. 'So you didn't manage to buy this house after all?'

'No, it's not for me, it's for my nephew, he's a nice chap. He's buying it, I thought you'd like to know that. But anyhow, I wanted you to have these,' and he brought his hands from behind his back to reveal a brace of pheasants, both plucked ready for the oven.

'Claude . . . you shouldn't.'

'No, I know I shouldn't, I know it's wrong to bribe the law, but this is not a bribe, not now you're leaving. It's a present for a friend. I just wanted to say thanks—you've allus been fair, got me out of a pickle or two, especially those times when Blaketon got his claws into me.'

'I'll buy you a drink next time I see you in the pub,' I said, accepting the pheasants.

But then I realized it was the close season for pheasants. Was he setting me up by giving me a pair of pheasants he'd poached from Lord Ashfordly's estate? For a fleeting moment, I felt very suspicious of Claude Jeremiah Greengrass, but as if reading my thoughts he smiled and said, 'They're clean, not nicked or poached, I didn't nick 'em from Whinstone Woods, they've been in a deep freezer since Christmas.'

'Thanks, Claude, not that I doubted you!'

'Aye, well, some might think wrong of me. But I must be off. I'm going to see a man about a dog. We'll meet again, Constable Nick, I'm sure. Or should it be Sergeant Nick now?'

'Just Nick will do nicely. See you, Claude. And thanks.'

And so he vanished to go about his business whatever it was, and I returned to my chores. I completed the inventory, swept the floors, locked all the doors and windows, and left.

I had my own car parked outside and so, en route to my new home in Maddleskirk, I stopped at the village shop and bought a bottle of champagne.

Tonight, Mary and I would celebrate the beginning of our new life.

* * *

With some surprise, I learned the piano had gone into Honeysuckle Cottage without any problems even if it had been tipped up on one end to manoeuvre it around corners. That meant it would need tuning once again, then I learned the removal men had had to take out the main bedroom window to fit in the dressing-table! Even without its legs and mirror, it wouldn't go up the narrow twisting staircase.

'Now we've got you in, Mr Rhea, I hope we don't have to move you out again,' said the driver as they were leaving.

'I hope we don't have to move you out of here,' said the thin one, and I gave them both a handsome tip. They'd probably be retired before we moved out of Honeysuckle Cottage.

It was a few months afterwards when I was enjoying a quiet drink with Mary in the lounge of the White Swan at Maddleskirk that I overheard a couple of old characters chatting in the bar. They were discussing me.

'Yon bobby from Aidensfield's gone to work in t'Training School at Police Headquarters at Northallerton,' said one. 'He's got his bairns into some posh schools and Ah'll never know how he manages that on a copper's wage, but he does write books and stuff, and he did get a footpath organized for t'hill before he left.'

'Did he, by gum? Well, that's summat useful for t'village. So what's he doing now?'

'They reckon it's a teaching job. Not real coppering or owt like that. He drives over there every day.'

'Which way does he go?'

The first pointed up to the moors and said, 'Over yon hill.'

THE END

ALSO BY NICHOLAS RHEA

Thank you for reading this book.

If you enjoyed it please leave feedback on Amazon or Goodreads, and if there is anything we missed or you have a question about, then please get in touch. We appreciate you choosing our book.

Founded in 2014 in Shoreditch, London, we at Joffe Books pride ourselves on our history of innovative publishing. We were thrilled to be shortlisted for Independent Publisher of the Year at the British Book Awards.

www.joffebooks.com

We're very grateful to eagle-eyed readers who take the time to contact us. Please send any errors you find to corrections@joffebooks.com. We'll get them fixed ASAP.

Lightning Source UK Ltd.
Milton Keynes UK
UKHW010109290822
407933UK00002B/281